Chapter One

IT WAS FOUR in the afternoon. A mild June rain cleansed the already immaculate Grosse Pointe sidewalks and nourished the fat green grass on the grounds of the three brick mansions at the end of a narrow cul-de-sac. These had been built in the twenties by men who founded automobile companies. Today they were all owned by Vittorio Tucci, although only one, the four story Federal-style mansion in the center, was occupied. The others stood empty but guarded, mute brick testimony to Vittorio Tucci's wish to be alone.

In the very center of the mansion, in a dimly lit, mahogany-paneled, windowless room, Vittorio Tucci sat sipping grappa and listening to Frank Sinatra's *Songs for Young Lovers*. He was seventy-four years old and dying.

Despite Tucci's love of privacy, there were seven people in

the house at that moment, each there to assure his physical safety and personal comfort. Such was the orderly nature of the household that he knew where every one of them was likely to be.

Johnny Baldini, once a sous-chef at "21" in New York, would be in the large kitchen in the rear of the house, along with his assistants, two Sicilian sisters of a certain age, distantly related to Don Vittorio. They were preparing the Tuesday meal: pasta primavera, chicken diavlo, and, lately, tiramisu. Over the years Don Vittorio had rarely indulged in dessert, just as he had seldom sipped grappa during working hours, but he was confident that alcohol and sweet, rich cream could do him no harm now that cancer was feasting on his blood. Don Vittorio was not indifferent to his imminent demise, but a lifetime of observation had taught him that every adversity had its benefits. Even death.

Still, he had no intention of dying in pain, which is why Joey Florio and a young nurse named Felice were on duty in the third-floor dispensary. Florio, whose father had been a member of the Tucci Family, had been put through medical school by the don. After his residency he became the Family doctor, dealing competently and discreetly with the Tuccis' various medical problems. There was a bed in the dispensary, and Vittorio imagined that Joey and Felice were in it now, making love, as they did every afternoon.

His information on Florio, like most of the information he received these days, was provided by his consigliere, Luigi Catello. Catello's domain was the basement, from which he had removed the bowling alley, the indoor pool, and the other entertainments of the mansion's former owner. He had replaced them with a secured electronic command-and-control center fit for a small NATO nation. From this listening post Catello maintained contact with the other Families and the politicians, judges, union bosses, journalists, stockbrokers, law-enforcement officers, and divines of various faiths with whom the Family did its business.

There was a guard on duty inside the house and three more outside, all supervised by Carlo Seluchi, commander of the afternoon shift, who sat in the security office on the second floor monitoring the closed-circuit TV screens that covered the grounds. It was on one of these screens that Seluchi saw Annette Tucci's black Lincoln Continental arrive at the gate, stop briefly, and then head down the private road in the direction of the house. He buzzed the don, two short rings to let him know that his daughter-in-law had arrived.

Don Vittorio heard the signal without enthusiasm. Twenty-five years earlier, when his son Roberto had married, he had been pleased. Annette was the daughter of Tommy "the Neck" Niccola, then a rising hood, now boss of Chicago. At the time, Don Vittorio was still fighting to consolidate his grip on Detroit and the alliance with such a feared man had been helpful. But now Detroit was at peace, Roberto was dead, and Don Vittorio had no further use for his shrewish, demanding daughter-in-law or her vulgar father.

Don Vittorio took a hard black Di Nobli from his humidor, lit it, and expelled a mouthful of acrid smoke. Annette hated the smell of cigars—she said it gave her cat, Scratch, a headache. Since this meeting was not one he was looking forward to, he hoped the air pollution would keep it short.

There was a soft knock, and Seluchi ushered Annette and her arrogant tan Abyssinian cat into the room. Annette wore black, as usual, but she didn't look like a grieving widow. Her dress was low-cut, exposing cleavage, tight across the hips, and short enough to show off her long, slender legs. Annette Tucci wasn't a beautiful woman—her skin was acne-scarred under her makeup, her nostrils were too large, and her jaw protruded slightly—but she was provocative and, now that her husband was dead, predatory.

The don knew this from personal experience. Several weeks after Roberto's funeral, Annette had propositioned him with an unemotional directness that shocked and impressed the old man. He had been tempted, too, although he turned her down. He let her think that he had refused out of a sense of propriety. In truth he was simply following his life-long practice of not getting into bed with a woman he feared.

Now Annette took a seat across the desk from the don, closed her brown eyes briefly, and said, "*Songs for Young Lovers*. Roberto's favorite. I had to play it for him in the hospital, over and over."

"I remember," said Don Vittorio. He remembered, too, that Annette hated Sinatra, which is why he had chosen him for today's soundtrack.

"How are you feeling?" she asked.

The don recognized this as a real question, not a pleasantry. He shrugged and raised his hands, palms up. There was no reason to pretend; Annette knew he was dying.

"You're going to have to choose someone to take your place," she said evenly. "It's time."

"Maybe I won't choose," said Don Vittorio. His voice was heavy, accented with just a touch of Sicily. "Maybe I'll just go to heaven and let Catello and Relli fight it out."

"That will never happen."

The don smiled, revealing a set of strong yellow teeth. "You don't think I'll go to heaven?"

Annette ignored the question. "This is a family business," she said. "It belonged to Roberto."

"Roberto is dead," said the don. "He died listening to Frank Sinatra."

"Roberto's heir is alive."

"Roberto's heir? A woman can't head a Family. That's the rule."

"It's a stupid rule," said Annette. "Women run corporations these days. You think I couldn't run the Tucci Family? I'm not as smart as Relli? Or as tough as Catello? Get outta here, I've lived my whole life with men like them."

Vittorio nodded at the justice of her remark; Annette Tucci was certainly capable of running the Family. She had a shrewd understanding of the realpolitik of their world—too shrewd, Vittorio knew, to imagine that she could actually become a don. And so he merely smiled and held up his manicured hands. "I don't make these rules," he said mildly.

"Fine, we go by the rules. According to the rules, the control belonged to Roberto," she said, fixing her father-in-law with a fierce glare. "Now it belongs to Bobby."

They stared at each other for a long moment, brown on brown. It was Vittorio who lowered his gaze first and chuckled. "How old is he?"

"Twenty-one. What were you doing when you were twenty-one?"

"Bobby's a sissy. He's got hair like a girl. He plays the guitar. Last Christmas he told me he wants to write novels, for Christ's sake. He wouldn't last ten minutes."

"He's got Tucci blood and Niccola blood. And he's got me. He'll do what I tell him."

The don had no doubt that his daughter-in-law was right; it would take a far stronger character than Bobby Tucci's to resist such a determined woman. "Even so, the men would never follow a boy," he said.

"They will if you say so."

"While I'm alive, yes. But afterward?" The don shook his head.

"If there's trouble, I can lean on my father."

"I see," said Tucci. Annette was telling him that if he refused to anoint Bobby, she'd use it as an excuse to start a war and bring her father in to take over Detroit.

In the old days Don Vittorio might have murdered his daughter-in-law, but now, in the face of his own mortality, he had no heart for committing mortal sins. He cleared his throat and said, "You would be putting your son at risk."

"That's what life's about, risk," said Annette. "Bobby

could crack up that Porsche you gave him. Or get himself shot in one of those nightclubs he plays in. Believe me, he'll be a lot safer where I can keep my eye on him. And once he makes his bones, the men will look after him."

"Jesus," muttered Don Vittorio, his voice a mixture of admiration and contempt. He had been right to fear this woman, a mother cold enough to make her son a murderer in the service of her own ambition.

"You know a man who doesn't make his bones will never get the respect," she said.

Don Vittorio acknowledged to himself that she was right. That was the rule. He leaned back in his padded chair and drew thoughtfully on his cigar. Suddenly he felt exhausted. "I'll consider it," he said.

Annette rose and gave her father-in-law a gaze of frank appraisal. "You better decide quick," she said. "No offense, Vittorio, but you're starting to smell like a bad oyster."

Chapter Two

BOBBY TUCCI LET himself in with his key. Tillie was in the living room of their small, off-campus apartment, curled up on the couch reading *Tender Is the Night* and eating ham-and-pineapple pizza. Bobby helped himself to a slice and plopped down next to her.

She put down her book and watched him take a huge bite of the pizza. "Debacle?" she asked.

"Fiasco," said Bobby. His voice was clear, a little ironic, his articulation the product of twelve years of prep school tinged by a stint as the lead singer in an R&B band.

"How was dinner?"

Bobby took another bite and said, "I couldn't get anything down."

"She must have loved that."

"Didn't even notice. I just pushed the food around on my plate. Meantime, she's tearing into her T-bone, socking down double martinis, and feeding Scratch Iranian caviar."

"My mother would freak if she took me out to dinner and I didn't eat."

"Mine doesn't freak, she freaks other people. You're not going to believe what she wants."

"I never believe anything you tell me about your mother," said Tillie. "The Madame Defarge of Grosse Pointe."

"More like Lady Macbeth," said Bobby. "She says it's time for me to learn about the family business. It's my, quote, goddamn birthright, unquote."

"She said that? 'Goddamn birthright'? You've got to let me meet her."

"It will never be," said Bobby with mock solemnity.

"I let you meet Big Sandy."

"Not the same," Bobby said. "Big Sandy's a gent."

"He's scared shit of you, that's all," said Tillie. This was true; Tillie's father was terrified of Bobby.

Bobby and Tillie had met junior year, in an American-lit seminar. She had been attracted by his lean body and long, sculpted fingers, his quirky curiosity, and the fact that he was the lead singer of Cold Duck, one of Ann Arbor's hottest bar bands. Bobby had been attracted to her for the same reason that every other guy on campus was, because she looked like Ali MacGraw in *Love Story*. "Only I've got better tits than Ali," she told him on their first date.

"How do you know that?"

Tucci shook his head. "They got dago turnkeys all over the joint, but there's no Yids. *Capisce?*"

Mendy nodded. "Yeah, but I ain't no teacher. I only got through the fourth grade."

"Hey, I don't want no college prep, just a few hundred words to rat-a-tat-tat with," said Tucci.

"There's fellas here born in the old country. They talk Yiddish way better than me," Mendy said.

"Yeah, but I want you."

"How come?"

"I been watchin' you. You got a pleasin' personality. I'll give you two cartons of smokes a week. We got a deal?"

"That'd be swell," Mendy said. Two cartons a week would make him rich.

They shook hands and Tucci said, "Before you start, take it to the Jew click, so it don't look like you're sellin' out the secret code."

"What if they say no dice?"

"You tell Abramsky that Vittorio Tucci's asking for a personal favor. And then you offer to split the smokes. That'll do it."

Tucci was right. "Just don't learn them *lokshen* too good," Bad Abe Abramsky instructed Mendy. "Enough so they can talk to each other, but not enough to understand us. *Fershteit?*"

At first Tucci's men called Mendy "Professore" and mocked the guttural sounds of Yiddish, but he won them over by teaching them a vocabulary they could appreciate:

goniff for thief, *curva* for hooker, *schtarke* for strong-arm man. Soon he had them gleefully calling one another *schmuck* and *dreck* and *mamzer* and refering to Mendy respectfully as the *melamed*—the teacher. Tucci gave him a different nickname: Mendy the Pearl.

NOW THE DON left Seluchi in the limo and went alone into the Bull Pen. The diner was closed and empty except for Mendy, who sat at the worn Formica counter sipping coffee. The two men embraced, and Mendy said, "You give me more warning, I would have whipped you up my spinach ravioli."

Tucci made no effort to feign disappointment. The Bull Pen was a popular gathering place for downtown types and nostalgic suburbanites, but it smelled of corned beef and pickles and, to the don's meticulous eye, appeared none too clean. He held Mendy at arm's length and said, "You're the worst cook in town, but you're lookin' good, I gotta admit."

It was true. Mendy's hair was white, slicked back, and fastened down by Yardley's pomade. His skin was smooth, his features well defined, and his expression boyishly open. Although he had a small gut, his body looked hard. He scrunched his eyes shut and ducked his head, but he didn't return his old friend's compliment.

The don wasn't surprised. Mendy the Pearl never lied except under oath, and telling the truth would have required him to say that Tucci looked awful. He had shrunk to Mendy's height. His thick olive skin was mottled and gray, he had gone bald, and his hands shook. Only his eyes and his voice were still strong. "How about a drink?" he said.

Mendy reached under the counter, brought out a bottle of Seagram's Seven, and poured three fingers into a chipped coffee mug—as a convicted felon he couldn't get a liquor license. He handed the mug to Tucci, raised his own cup and said, "*Salud.*"

"*L'chayim,*" the don replied.

They sat down and Tucci said, "You remember Annette? Roberto's wife?"

Mendy raised his eyebrows affirmatively. Nobody forgot Annette Tucci.

"The other day she come to me with a proposal. I want your opinion."

Mendy sat silently while Tucci recounted his conversation with Annette. When he was finished, Mendy said, "Whew!"

"Yeah," Tucci said. "So? Whaddya think?"

Mendy shrugged. In forty years, Vittorio Tucci had never once solicited his opinion except as a prelude to asking a favor. Mendy didn't resent this. He knew his limitations. There was no reason for a brilliant man like the don to seek his counsel.

Tucci said, "She puts out the word Bobby's next in line, and I won't even be cold before somebody whacks him. Relli might not even wait *that* long. Then that no-neck old man of hers steps in and plants the Niccola flag in Detroit."

"She'd do that to her own kid?"

"Remember Lottie LaScuzz?"

Mendy nodded. Lottie had been a Hamtramck madam who put her three daughters to work at a Dodge Motors whorehouse screwing autoworkers. When one ran away, she assured the loyalty of the others by hooking them on heroin. Lottie had been dead for years, but she lived on in the memories of old-timers like Mendy and Don Vittorio, a reminder of the unreliability of maternal devotion.

"I don't wanna see my Family go to those fuckin' Niccolas," said Tucci.

"You gonna go to war?"

Tucci sighed. "Look at me. Do I look like I can go to fuckin' war?" He lowered his voice and said, "My goddamn memory's shot. Half the time I forget what people tell me."

A look of genuine concern spread over Mendy's face. "Jeez," he said, "that's lousy."

"Yeah, well. I can cover it up good enough to handle my business, but I'm not in shape to fight a war. I'd rather turn the whole thing over to one of the New York Families, let them deal with it after I'm gone. Only—"

"What?"

"Annette got me thinkin'. Maybe Bobby *does* deserve a shot. I mean, we're not talkin' about peanuts here."

"He's a college boy," said Mendy.

"Yeah, but he's a Tucci. He's got the blood. What I wonder is, does he have the heart? Which is where you come in."

Mendy held up a handful of crooked, broken fingers and said, "Hey, I'm retired."

Tucci waved dismissively. "Nobody's talkin' about a

comeback," he said. "Just meet the kid, sound him out like. Tell him some of your bullshit stories about the old days, see how he reacts."

"Jeez, why don't you just talk to him direct?"

"Cause *I* ain't retired," said Tucci. "He starts asking me questions, maybe he shouldn't know the answers. *You* talk to him, see if the kid's got any larceny in his soul. If he ain't, no harm done. But if he's got a taste for it—"

"I got two priors," said Mendy. "One more felony, I go back to the joint for life."

Tucci took Mendy's hand in his, pulled him close, and said, "You think I'd get you in dutch? After all we been through together?"

"Aw," said Mendy, embarrassed.

"Damn right, 'Aw,'" said Tucci. He looked deeply into Mendy's eyes and said, "I pledge to you I won't do nothin' to get you involved. You understand?"

Mendy held the stare for a long moment. All his professional life he had been lied to by bosses; it was his inability to know when and why that had kept him from an executive career of his own. Vittorio Tucci was a boss, but he was also a friend. Mendy blinked and nodded. "Okay," he said. "I'll talk to the kid."

Tucci gave Mendy a lipless grin and patted his arm. He saw the skepticism in the Pearl's eyes, but it didn't worry him. Sicilians talked about loyalty all day long, but there wasn't one of them who wouldn't sell his mother. Mendy Pearlstein was the only truly loyal man he had ever met.

That was why Vittorio needed him. If Bobby had the makings, Mendy was the only one he'd trust to initiate the boy. Mendy, despite the life sentence hanging over his head, would never roll over on the kid. And there was something else. He could rely on Mendy to teach his grandson how to make his bones without falling in love with it.

ALBERTO RELLI PULLED his four-year-old black Eldorado into the service bay of Cady Brothers Car Stereo & Sound, off Gratiot. The car seemed plain next to the other vehicles in the lot—a Rolls Silver Cloud and a gold custom-made van whose vanity plate read FLY. Relli didn't care that his car was drab. He had other ways of making an impression.

There were three men with Relli. One stayed behind the wheel; the other two followed him into the squat brick shop. R&B blared from huge speakers. Four young black men dressed in striped bell-bottoms, neon silk shirts, platform shoes, and wide-brimmed Superflies lounged near the counter, moving to the thud of the bass. Cady Brothers was sound merchant to Detroit's most musically discriminating pimps and drug dealers.

Relli saw Solomon Cady behind the counter. Cady was in his early twenties, an Iraqi Christian weight lifter who sometimes worked as a bodyguard for visiting rock stars. A few months earlier he had borrowed $50,000 from a Tucci loan shark, and now he owed $125,000.

Relli walked briskly to Cady and, in a fluid motion, hit him across the head with a tire iron. Cady staggered and fell. Relli went around the counter, kicked him in the head, and began dragging him by his feet toward the soundproof listening room in the rear of the shop. The whole thing took less than thirty seconds.

The black guys at the counter glanced at Relli's men, who were holding sawed-off shotguns. "Looks like y'all got business," said one. "That's cool, we'll swing back around later."

One of Relli's men locked the door behind them and hung the OUT TO LUNCH sign. The other went into the soundproof demo room where Relli was binding Cady's hands and legs with telephone wire. Blood ran from the gash in Cady's skull, but he was conscious.

"I told you to pay back the money by the first of the month," said Relli. He was around forty-five, not short and not tall, with a wiry body, strong, hairy arms, irregular features, and, already at noon, a heavy five o'clock shadow. He spoke with a flat Michigan accent. "You operating on some kind of special A-rab calendar or what?"

"Fuck you," said Cady.

Relli dragged Cady over to the largest set of speakers, placed one against each side of Cady's head and secured them with wire, like huge electronic earmuffs. "I talked but you didn't listen," Relli said. "You turned a deaf ear. Or maybe you got a problem with your hearing?"

"Fuck you," Cady said again, but this time his voice shook.

"We're gonna do an experiment," said Relli. "A hearing test." He put a Sly Stone cassette in the master tape deck and began pressing buttons. When he found what he was looking for he slipped in a pair of earplugs and tossed a pair to his man, whose name was John Bertoia. Then he said to Cady, "Listen to this. Tell me how it sounds to you." He gave the volume dial a vicious twist. Cady's scream, as his eardrums shattered, was drowned out by ten thousand decibels of "Everyday People."

Bertoia watched in admiration as Cady writhed in pain. After a minute or so, Relli abruptly turned off the sound, leaving a silence almost as loud as the music.

"Did you get that?" Relli hollered to Cady. Then he hit full volume again. Cady twitched in agony. Tears ran down his face. Relli gave him a look of cold contempt and left him jerking on the floor, the music crashing against his ruined ears.

THEY WERE BACK in the Cadillac, heading down Gratiot toward the far East Side, before the ringing in Bertoia's head subsided enough for him to speak. "I never heard of nobody slammin' a guy like that, using stereo speakers," he said. "You think it up yourself?"

"I came up with it watching the eggplants out on Belle Isle, the big radios they walk around with," said Relli. "I figured, hey."

Bertoia and the others shook their heads with appreciation for Relli's ingenuity.

"You keep your eyes open, you get ideas," Relli said.

Relli dropped Bertoia and the others at the Palermo Inn, popped some Dean Martin into the tape deck, and headed for the freeway. He was running late for his meeting with Luigi Catello, the consigliere. Relli liked to be early for meetings; getting there first gave him an advantage. Especially when the venue was a new spot.

It was like Catello to have chosen a Big Boy restaurant on the other side of town. The sensitive nature of the meeting dictated that it be held out of the way—Relli accepted that—but he didn't see why they had to meet in a fucking Big Boy. He worked hard all day long, and he looked forward to his meals. That was one of the differences between a warrior like himself and a desk jockey like Catello.

Relli and Catello were about the same age, and they had been rivals ever since Relli joined the Family as a young recruit during the Mossi war of 1954. The war eventually consolidated Tucci control over southern Michigan all the way down to the Ohio border, but when Relli signed up the outcome was still very much in doubt. Vittorio Tucci was in active command of his troops, which were outnumbered and outgunned by the men of Don Silvio Mossi of Cleveland.

Relli had been assigned to a search-and-destroy squad

that roamed the city looking for Mossi targets of opportunity. Soon his skill and daring came to the attention of Don Vittorio himself, who made a point of publicly praising the young soldier. When Relli caught a Mossi captain in a roadhouse near Monroe and brought him in as a hostage, the don, in an almost unprecedented gesture, asked him to dinner at his own table. The don's son, Roberto, invited him to join his regime as an underboss. It was a wartime rank, but even so, Tucci Family veterans could not recall a more meteoric rise.

It was at this dinner that Relli first met Luigi Catello, who scurried in and out of the room several times, whispering in the don's ear. Relli had heard of him—Catello was Don Vittorio's driver—but this was the first time he had actually seen him, and he wasn't impressed. Catello was short and round, with a soft-looking middle and narrow shoulders. His hair, which he combed straight back, was already thinning, and he wore horn-rims. Catello's most noteworthy feature, though, was a pair of large, rubbery lips. All in all he reminded Relli of his grandmother's gnocchi, and that was the nickname he silently gave him.

And yet it was Catello, the Gnocchi, who had eventually come up with the master stroke that won the war for the Tucci Family—an idea so brilliant that even today, twenty years later, Relli recalled it with a combination of awe and jealousy. And although Catello had never again demonstrated such imagination and daring, that one time had been enough to put him permanently ahead of Relli on the Family's advancement track.

Catello, in those days, was a quiet, unassuming young

man with impeccable credentials—his grandfather and Don Vittorio's father had come to America from the same Sicilian village—which is why he had been entrusted with the highly sensitive job of wartime chauffeur. More than once he had sat silently at the wheel while, in the backseat, Don Vittorio discussed strategy and tactics with Roberto. He knew the Tuccis were losing the war, and one day he broke his silence.

"From what I hear, Don Silvio is a rare Man of Honor," he said. "Devout. Virtuous. A loving father to his children."

The description was accurate, and it annoyed Vittorio. "Maybe you oughta go work for him," he growled.

Catello was unfazed by the sarcasm. "Don Silvio has three children," he said. "The oldest boy, Frank, is sick with polio. The other one, Pietro, is a priest. The way it looks, neither one's gonna produce any kids."

"So what?"

"Don Silvio's also got a sixteen-year-old daughter, Maria. They call her Margie. She's in school with the sisters out West in Arizona. She's got bad asthma."

"Mossi's personal problems are none of my concern."

"The way I see it, he's got an awful lot riding on the little girl. She don't make him grandchildren, that's the end of his bloodline."

"What should I do, find her a husband?" asked Tucci impatiently.

"Snatch her," said Catello.

"You're outta your fuckin' mind," said Tucci. "Civilians are off limits."

Catello shrugged. "What's a civilian? When Truman

dropped the A-bomb nobody beefed, 'cause it stopped the war. Same here. Snatch the girl, the war ends."

"And as soon as I let her go, it starts all over again, only this time I got every Family in the country pissed off at me for violating the rules."

"Not if Don Silvio makes the peace."

"He'd never do it. I take his kid, he can't forgive that."

"Maybe not. But if you return the girl in the right condition, he's gonna have his hands tied."

Two months later, a despairing Don Silvio received a visitor from Detroit. The emissary was Catello.

He spoke in Sicilian dialect to underscore the solemnity of his message. "Don Vittorio wants you to know while our Families are at war, that is business. He has been miserable over your personal misfortune. He has used all the powers at his command to find your missing daughter. And he has succeeded."

Tears of relief welled up in Don Silvio's eyes. "Thank God."

"Maria is alive and safe. But"—Catello's voice faltered—"I regret to tell you that she is pregnant."

The blood drained from Don Silvio's face. His mouth worked, but no words came out. Finally he managed to mutter, "Maria is a virgin."

"She was raped," said Catello. "She fought for her virtue with all her might, but she was overpowered. Rest assured that the men who did this have been punished."

"Men?" It was a hoarse whisper. "There was more than one?"

Catello reached into a leather briefcase and extracted a dozen snapshots. They were the faces of rough-looking young men, five black, six white, one Chinese. "These are the rapists," he said. "Unfortunately we don't know which one of them is the father."

The word "father" made Don Silvio wince as if he had been slapped in the face. He put his head in his hands and wept. When he raised his eyes, he saw the sly smile on Catello's fat, round lips and he knew the truth. Catello wanted him to know. His instinct was to fly at the bespectacled man, to tear his tongue from his mouth. But Maria was still a captive. Mustering all his self-control, Don Silvio said, "Bring me my daughter."

"Don Vittorio thinks it best that she not return home just yet. After all, this is a delicate matter. It must be handled with discretion."

"Don Vittorio has thought of everything," said Silvio Mossi. Blood was pounding at his temples, yet he managed to keep his voice level.

"There is also the matter of your grandchild to consider," said Catello. His dropped his gaze to the gallery of faces arrayed on the table before them. "We could, of course, make certain medical arrangements—"

"*Infamita!*" exclaimed Don Silvio. As Catello had guessed, abortion was out of the question.

"In that case, the birth must take place, in utmost secrecy, and the child be given away. Don Vittorio will be honored to make the arrangement."

"I am capable of taking care of my own daughter," said Don Silvio.

"Don Vittorio feels that a father should not be asked to make such an arrangement for his own daughter. Especially since outrage might impair a father's judgment."

"What do you mean?"

"No man, especially not such a man as yourself, could allow his daughter to be violated without thirsting for retribution. That is only natural. But such an impulse, noble as it is, would be disastrous. Should you take any action, word would inevitably get out that your daughter has been ruined, that she is the mother of a bastard child. Then she would have no prospects for marriage—and you would die without a proper heir."

Don Silvio went to the window and peered at Lake Erie in the distance. Then he sighed heavily and said, "I will do as Don Vittorio wishes."

"He will treat your daughter as his own," said Catello. "The story will be that she spent a year in a convent. She failed to communicate with you out of a childishly devout belief that she must be cut off from the world. An accommodating mother superior will corroborate this. There will be no scandal."

"I see," said Don Silvio. He went back into English and said, "What does Don Vittorio want in return for all this kindness?"

"Only an end to the war."

"On what terms?"

Catello permitted himself a fleeting smile. "His."

Once again, Don Silvio sighed. Someday he would take his revenge, but for now there was no choice. "Yes," he said. "I agree. Please tell Don Vittorio that I won't forget his kindness."

"I'm sure you won't," said Catello. He reached into his briefcase and took out a reel of film. "There are only two copies. Don Vittorio has one; he wants you to have the other. As a token of his esteem." He paused and added, "It features your daughter."

Wordlessly, Don Silvio accepted the film. He had been wondering how Tucci dared risking his anger. Now he knew.

When Roberto learned of Catello's mission he was furious. "You made a pact with the devil," he told his father. "Someday it will come back and destroy us all." Relli was Roberto's protégé, and that was enough to make him Catello's enemy.

Still, there was little Relli could do, and he had never quite caught up with Catello. He was highly appreciated and well paid by the Tucci Family, but a generation of peace had diminished the status of martial virtues. Over time he had become reconciled to the fact that in the placid, businesslike postwar world of the Tuccis, he had risen as high as a warrior could.

Then Roberto dropped dead of a stroke at the concession stand during the second period of a Wings game, and the don himself came down with cancer, and suddenly the settled world of the Tuccis was in flux.

Don Vittorio's time was rumored to be short, and he had no successor. Relli figured that Catello would exploit his inside position to win the don's blessing. If he did, the moment Tucci was dead it would be war—and in a war, Alberto Relli's military skills would prevail.

Relli saw the Big Boy sign up ahead. He pulled into the crowded lot, scowling when he spotted Catello's Cadillac already parked near the door. The restaurant was full of young guys from the nearby office towers, junior executives in wash-and-wear white shirts eating ground round while the bosses and their secretaries were down the street at Excalibur putting two hundred bucks' worth of wine and sirloin on the company tab. He spotted Catello at a rear table, reading a newspaper, a gnocchi with bifocals.

"How the Tigers do last night?" he asked, slipping into a seat across from the consigliere.

"Stock page," said Catello, tapping the paper.

Relli snorted. He could never understand how wiseguys who wouldn't even consider betting on an honest horse race could get taken in by the Protestant shell game conducted daily on Wall Street.

A waitress in a starched white uniform set two laminated menus on the bare tabletop. "You got a wine list?" Relli asked.

The waitress, a thirtyish woman with a honey-colored beehive, ample breasts, and a mouthful of spearmint, gave him a look.

The consigliere fixed his rubber lips into a smile and said,

"I'll have the Swankie Frankie, double fries, and a Coke. And an order of onion rings."

"Water," said Relli tightly. "In a clean glass." The waitress gave him another look. This time he gave her one back. She dropped her eyes and fled.

"Nervous broad," said Relli.

"She's got her job to do," said Catello.

"What are you, bangin' her?"

Catello's brown eyes blinked solemnly behind the thick lenses. "I invited you to lunch because we need to talk," he said. "But if it's gonna be this way, why don't you get up and leave?"

Relli surprised Catello by smiling. "I didn't realize it was you inviting me," he said. "I thought we was goin' dutch." He signaled for the waitress, who returned with obvious reluctance. "What's good here?" he asked.

"Everything."

"Yeah? Okay, bring me everything."

"What do you mean?"

"Take the menu and gimme one of everything that's on it," said Relli. "To go. Wrap it all up. And a piece of cherry pie and coffee for here."

"You're kidding," the waitress said.

Relli gave her a cold smile and said, "Do I look like the kinda guy kids around in the fuckin' Big Boy?"

She stared at him, saying nothing.

"What're you, deaf?" said Relli. "Jesus, is everybody in the fuckin' city deaf?"

"Go ahead," said Catello quietly. Bertoia had already phoned him with a report on what Relli had done to Solomon Cady. Catello wasn't banging the waitress, but the idea had crossed his mind, and he had no intention of allowing her to wind up with shattered eardrums. "Wrap it up and give me the bill."

Relli picked up a laminated menu and began reading, his lips moving as he ran his finger down the price list. Finally he said, "Seven hundred and fifty bucks, give or take. Let's find out what's worth seven-fifty to talk about, far as you're concerned."

"The future of the Family," said Catello. "What happens after Don Vittorio dies."

"Don Vittorio will live for many years," said Relli formally. He was well aware that Catello made a practice of recording his conversations.

"Hopefully, yes," said the consigliere. "But let's be practical. He's got cancer. How much longer can he have?" It was a rhetorical question. Dr. Florio was on Catello's payroll, so he knew the answer: six months at the outside.

"However long it is, you and me are gonna be on opposite sides after the funeral," said Relli.

Catello said, "You ever hear of Benjamin Franklin?"

"Sure," said Relli. "The guy who invented the kite."

"He said, 'We hang together or we hang separate.' "

"Meaning what?"

"Meaning that we got problems with Chicago," said Catello. "Annette wants this thing for her old man. She's gonna open up the door."

"Get outta here."

"Hey," said Catello. He fell silent as the waitress arrived with his meal and Relli's pie and coffee. Relli waited for her to leave and said, "Let's say you're right, we got an Annette problem. I don't see why you're gonna tell me about it. You got an answer to that, I wanna hear it."

Catello swallowed and dabbed his lips. "For right now I just wanna call your attention," he said. "Things are gonna start happening in the Family. Sooner or later you're gonna realize it. Then we can sit down and figure out how to work together."

"Say you're right again—what am I gonna need you for?"

"Information," said Catello. "Just like you don't know about Annette and I do? It's gonna be the same right down the line. I got sources of information. You fly blind in a situation like this, you get whacked. I'm the eyes."

Relli took a bite of cherry pie and thought it over. Catello was a master fucking spy, no question; he could never compete with the consigliere for military intelligence. "Okay," he said, "put the question backwards. You got these sharp eyes, whaddya need me for?"

"Tommy Niccola comes in to help Annette after the don dies, it's war. I can't win a war against him and you at the same time. Same for you. That's why we gotta be on the same side."

"Yeah, and when it's over we beat each other's brains in," said Relli. "So what's the point?"

Catello looked at Relli for a long moment and then said, "I'm playing my cards face up here. We beat Niccola, you and me could have a problem. But it don't have to be that way. You got any idea how big the Tucci Family really is?"

Relli smiled knowingly. Actually he had no idea about many of the Family's activities, but he wasn't about to admit it.

"Okay," said Catello. "Then you know there's plenty here for both of us. When the don goes, I want the legal businesses. I don't have the muscle for the street stuff. Take it all, the gambling, the hookers, the smuggling, the protection, the unions, it's yours."

"You didn't mention the drugs," said Relli. "What'd they do, legalize cocaine and I didn't hear about it?"

"Drugs we gotta split," said Catello. "There's too much money in it for just one or the other. We buy together, you get the wholesale and the street business, and I do the laundering through one of our banks. We can work out the percentages later."

"Jesus, you got this all figured out," said Relli. "You take this and I get that, like it's your call."

"Come on, Alberto, you want to run an insurance company? Or a savings and loan? The split's fair. I want you happy. Otherwise the deal's no good anyway."

"Who gets to be the don?"

"You want it, you got it," said Catello. "To me it's an old-fashioned title."

Relli regarded Catello with contempt; only a gnocchi would think such a thing. It was Catello's lack of honor and manliness that made his proposition believable. Relli thought it over and decided there was no harm in going along—for a while. Sooner or later an enemy would surface—Tommy Niccola, the New York Families, Catello himself with hired muscle, it didn't really matter. Relli had absolute confidence that when the time came, he had the balls and the brains to beat all comers. He signaled for the waitress. "You got my order ready?" he demanded.

"There's eighteen main courses on that menu," she said.

"Well, I changed my mind," said Relli, standing. "I just want the pie and the coffee. My friend will take care of it." He turned and walked away. The waitress called after him, but he kept going.

"You already working on that order?" Catello asked.

"They're bagging up the salads and the desserts back there right now," said the waitress. "Everything else is on the grill or in the oven. Sorry, but you're gonna have to pay for it."

"I got an idea," said Catello. "Let's sell it."

"Used food?"

"Who's gonna know? Peddle the stuff to customers. Whatever you sell, great, you keep ten percent. The rest I'll spring for. What time you get off?"

"This isn't some kind of Health Department sting, is it?"

Catello reached into his pocket and extracted a wad of hundred-dollar bills held together by a rubber band. He peeled off two and handed them to her. "I'm your first customer," he said. "Salads and pies for everybody, pass 'em around."

The waitress smiled for the first time. "I get off at six."

"Great, I'll see you then. And whatever the bill comes to, bring me a receipt."

"A receipt? What for?"

"The IRS," said Catello. "This was a business lunch. It's deductible."

Chapter Five

BOBBY SPOTTED MENDY Pearlstein as soon as he walked through the door. It wasn't hard. There were maybe two hundred people packed into Trailers, a club in downtown Ann Arbor. Among the townies and a smattering of students Mendy stood out; no one else was wearing a straw Panama, a yellow sport jacket, a white tie on a black shirt, or a pair of black-and-white shoes.

From the bandstand Bobby watched Mendy say something to Eddie, the bartender. Eddie laughed, took Mendy's hat, and poured him a drink. Bobby was impressed by how relaxed the old guy looked. He'd seen plenty of old people come into clubs; mostly they hung around for a minute or two with an uncomfortable expression on their faces and then split. The ones who stayed got plastered and acted pissed-off at everybody else for being young. But this guy just leaned against the bar like it was his regular spot, sipping a whiskey and moving his head to the beat of "Driving Wheel." Bobby decided he must be a promoter or a club owner.

At the break Bobby went over and introduced himself. They shook hands, and Mendy said, "Jeez, you guys are terrific."

Bobby nodded his thanks and said, "We can talk in the back, it's quieter." He led Mendy to a table where Tillie was sitting. "Mr. Pearlstein likes what we're doing," he told her.

"Call me Mendy."

Tillie looked him over dubiously. The rock business was full of weirdos, but this one looked like a character out of *Guys and Dolls*.

Mendy signaled for a round of drinks and said, "What do you call your combo?"

Bobby kept his smile to himself and said, "Cold Duck. We do a lot of our own stuff and some R&B classics—Little Johnny Taylor, Hank Ballard, Little Willie John—"

"Poor Willie," said Mendy. "He was a nice kid, but he had a complex about his height. Died in the joint."

"You knew Little Willie John?"

"Sure," said Mendy. "I had a spot near the old Flame Show Bar, the Greenwood Inn. Willie used to drop by every now and then." He closed his eyes tightly, concentrating. "I guess that would have been about 1950, give or take a year."

"A nightclub?" asked Bobby.

"Nah, it was a gin mill," said Mendy. "For hillbillies

mostly. That place was so tough I had a guy working in the basement full-time just repairing the furniture."

Tillie giggled; she was stoned. "You're just making that up," she said.

"Aw," said Mendy.

"You ever manage any R&B acts?" Bobby asked.

"Closest I ever came was this one time, I won fifteen percent of Jackie Wilson shooting craps."

"*The* Jackie Wilson?"

"He wasn't big back then. I traded my share of him to a bookie named One-Eye Finkel for a used DeSoto."

The drinks arrived and Mendy raised his glass. "Here's to the memory of Willie John," he said. "May God bless him wherever he's at."

A pudgy young black man with a puffy Afro came up and said, "Hey, Bobby, starting time."

Bobby said, "This is our drummer, Carver Cleveland."

"You got a nice hand," said Mendy.

Cleveland said, "Thanks. Come on, baby, they don't pay no overtime in this place."

Tillie watched Bobby go up to the small stage. Then she turned to Mendy and said, "What kind of shows do you put on?"

"Me? I never put on a show in my life. I've got a little diner down by the ballpark. The Bull Pen Deli."

"Bobby thinks you're a promoter."

Mendy opened his brown eyes wide and said, "Jeez, what gave him that idea?"

"You know Bobby's mother, don't you?" said Tillie with stoned insight.

Mendy nodded.

"She's the one who sent you over here, I bet."

"Annette? Nah, I haven't spoken to her since just after Roberto died. Bobby's dad."

"So what, you just happened to stumble in the door?"

"Aw," said Mendy. "Bobby's grampa told me about him and I decided to catch his act."

"Bobby know that? That his grandfather sent you?"

"I didn't get a chance to tell him, is all."

"But you will?"

"Course."

Bobby played a blues riff and began to sing a slow song about his best friend's woman. "This is one he wrote," said Tillie.

Mendy nodded, rose, and held out his hand. "Would you care to dance?"

There was no dance floor in the Trailer. Here and there people swayed in their seats, but no one was on their feet. Tillie giggled. "Sure, why not?"

Mendy took Tillie in an old-fashioned clutch, right arm around her waist, left arm extended. She was an inch or two taller than he was, but he held her easily and firmly, leading her with surprising grace through a step she guessed was the fox-trot. They danced between the tables in the back of the room, Mendy's smooth cheek pressed against hers. "You got a nice light step," he said.

"And you used to dance with Ginger Rogers, right?" They both laughed.

"Hey, watch it, gramps, you bumped my arm," a voice said. Mendy turned and saw a beefy townie in his late twenties, with a red crew cut and a puddle of spilled beer on the table in front of him.

Mendy said, "Sorry, buddy."

"Yeah, buddy," said one of the men sitting with the crew cut. There were three of them, and they were drunk.

"Hey, you fucked up his tuxedo," said the other. "Least you can do is pay the cleaning bill."

"Aw, let's just have a good time," said Mendy.

"He your sugar daddy? You make him take his teeth out before he goes down on you?" said the crew cut.

"That's not the right kind of language to use in front of a lady," said Mendy evenly.

"What you gonna do, wash my mouth out with soap?"

Tillie made eye contact with Eddie the bartender. She saw him move around the bar, and she said, "Big ugly motherfucker. I bet you killed little babies in Vietnam, didn't you, you muscle-bound chicken shit."

The crew cut clambered to his feet, but Eddie intercepted him. "Time to leave, fellas," he said calmly. They looked at the Colt .45 in Eddie's left hand, climbed noisily out of their seats, and swaggered out the door.

"Sorry," said Eddie. He knew who Bobby's grandfather was.

"You done that like a pro," Mendy said to him.

"Thanks. I'll send you over some drinks."

They went back to their table. "You all right?" asked Tillie.

Mendy blinked. "You got quite a way with words."

Tillie leaned over and kissed him on the cheek. "You're adorable, you know that?" Grass and adrenaline had given her a very nice buzz.

Mendy smiled and put his arm around her shoulder. "You ain't bad either, toots," he said. "You're the berries."

The last set ended at one. "How about we hit a blind pig somewheres?" Mendy suggested.

"What's that?" asked Tillie.

"It's what you call an after-hours joint."

"Blind pig," repeated Bobby. "Cool expression."

"Let's just go back to our place," said Tillie. "It stays open all night, and the booze is already paid for."

"You go ahead," Bobby said. "I'll give Carver a hand breaking down the equipment and meet you at home."

Tillie followed Mendy into the parking lot. Ten yards away the crew cut, a quart bottle of Blatz in his hand, was urinating on her van.

"Get away from there, you asshole," she snapped.

The crew cut turned and faced them.

"And put that thing in your pants."

"You put it in."

Mendy said, "Aw, buddy, it's late. Why don't you just go home?"

"Why don't you suck my dick, grampa?" He waved the bottle drunkenly.

Bobby walked out of the bar carrying his Fender in a leather case. "What's going on?" he asked.

"Hey, it's Fabian," said the crew cut.

Bobby made no reply. He had an expression on his face that Mendy couldn't read.

"Let's take a ride," the crew cut said to Tillie.

She shot him the finger and said, "Take a ride on this."

The crew cut took a step forward and said, "You talk like a five-dollar whore, you know that? Is that what you cost, five dollars?"

Bobby stepped in front of Tillie.

"What's your problem, Fabian? Five bucks ain't enough?"

Bobby said, "Hey, I don't want any trouble." His left hand was outstretched, beseeching. His right held the Fender by the neck.

"Too fucking bad," the crew cut said. He moved toward Tillie. Bobby swung in a short arc. The guitar hit the crew cut on the side of the head with a thump, like a baseball bat smashing a pumpkin. He crumpled to the asphalt.

"Cocksucker, I'll get you for this," the crew cut mumbled.

Bobby knelt down next to him. "Fuck with me and I'll kill you. I'm telling you this in all sincerity." Then he slapped him across the face, bringing tears to his eyes.

Mendy blinked and swallowed hard. He had something to report to Don Vittorio. His grandson was a Tucci.

Chapter Six

MENDY PUT A dish of scrambled eggs and salami in front of Bobby. It was four in the morning, and the Bull Pen Deli was empty. They had dropped Tillie off, but Bobby had been too wired to sleep. He and Mendy had driven down to Detroit together, Bobby gunning his Porsche up to 110 and talking nonstop.

Bobby ate a forkful of eggs and said, "Hey, not bad. Where did you learn to cook like this?"

"Jackson."

"Mississippi?"

"Prison. I learned in the joint."

"What were you in for? I mean, if you don't mind saying." It was the kind of question he had been raised never to ask.

Mendy shrugged. "Nah, that's okay. Which time?"

"How many times were there?"

"Two," Mendy said. "Once for firebombing cleaning plants back in the thirties and another time for boosting some jewels. I did a couple years when I was a kid, too, but I don't count that 'cause it was juvenile farm. Hey, you want something to drink?"

"Maybe coffee," Bobby said.

"I'd skip the coffee if I was you," Mendy said. "You're het up enough already."

"I haven't hit anyone since grade school," Bobby said. "I've never been in a real fight in my life."

"Well, you showed good stuff," said Mendy. "I got a bottle of Seagram's, you want a snort?"

"I'd rather smoke a joint," said Bobby, extracting one from his shirt pocket. "If it's cool with you."

Mendy frowned. Bobby said, "Hey, it's a lot better for you than booze."

"Aw, it's not that," said Mendy. "I just don't think it's such a hot idea, you walkin' around with drugs in your pocket."

"What are they going to do, arrest me for possession of a couple joints? They'd have to lock up the whole campus."

Mendy shrugged. "You're not a regular college boy. You gotta be more careful."

"'Cause my last name is Tucci?" said Bobby, lighting the joint.

"You got a lot of your grandfather in you, y'know?"

"You two are old friends, huh?" said Bobby.

"We was in prison together, my first stretch. He was up

47

there for, I think, armed robbery. Yeah, I know him pretty good."

"I hardly know him at all," said Bobby.

"That's too bad. More eggs?"

"No, thanks. Can I ask you something?"

"Go ahead."

"It's personal."

"Hey."

"Are you in the mafia?"

"Nah," said Mendy. "There ain't no Jews in the mafia. Besides, I'm retired."

"But you were a mobster."

"Oh, sure."

"A boss like my grandfather?"

Mendy laughed. "I'm a knock-around fella," he said. "You're grampa's a brilliant man."

"That's one word for it," said Bobby.

Mendy frowned. "You look around Detroit these days, you see a mess. But when your grampa was coming up, this place was hopping. Booze coming across from Canada, cars rolling out of the factories, money everywhere. I bet there was five hundred cathouses and carpet joints downtown. Nightspots, fancy restaurants, burlesque houses, opium dens—"

"Opium dens?"

"Sure, in Chinatown." Mendy shut his eyes for a moment, a sweet memory animating his face. "We used to boost cars down there on Saturday nights and sell 'em back to their owners on Monday. See, back then they didn't have no auto-theft insurance."

Bobby laughed.

"Seriously," said Mendy. "In those days everybody wanted a piece of Detroit. Lansky, Luciano, Capone, all of 'em. Henry Ford had his own private army under Harry Bennett. Then later there was the union guys like Hoffa. The biggest hoods in America fought over this city, but it was your grampa who walked away with the pie. Hey, speaking of pie, you want some? I got apple and blueberry."

"No, thanks," said Bobby. All his life he had avoided the secrets of the Tuccis. Now here was Mendy the Pearl revealing them with the blithe unconcern of a man gossiping over the back fence. "I wonder how many people my grandfather had to kill to get his pie."

Mendy gave Bobby a mild look and said, "There's no statute of limitations on that."

"Meaning what?"

"Lemme tell you a story," said Mendy, resting his elbows on the counter and assuming a confidential tone. "There's a guy used to come in here every morning for breakfast. Back in Pro'bition he did the job for the Purple Gang on a *sthinker* named Hyman Rivkin. A *sthinker* means a stool pigeon in Yiddish.

"Anyways, this guy got caught and spent years in the joint. When he come out he liked to have his breakfast here, shooting the breeze with the guys. He was a nice fella, good sense of humor, and he knew a million stories."

"Just your average, ordinary murderer," said Bobby.

Mendy shook his head. "What the hell, he paid the price. He was entitled, y'know? Anyways, about five years ago a story gets published in the paper. Some professor says he found out that, back in the thirties, a warden up at Jackson let a guy out one night to do a mob hit on a Detroit police captain.

"That morning this guy I mentioned comes in for break-fast. One of the other fellas asks him wasn't he up at Jackson at the time? This guy just gets up and walks out. That was the last time he ever came in here. I see him around the neigh-borhood. He's eighty years old, but he still dresses sharp as a tack. Has his breakfast someplace else, I guess."

"You're saying this guy is the one who killed the police captain?"

Mendy shrugged. "Nah, I doubt it. But see, since there's no statute of limitations on murder, that's the one subject that talking about it don't make sense."

"In other words my grandfather's a murderer but you don't want to say so."

"You want some more eggs?"

"I guess you'd say it's just business."

Mendy sighed and said, "Tonight, when you smacked that guy with your guitar, you coulda killed him, y'know?"

"That's different. It was self-defense."

"Self-defense? He never even laid a hand on you."

"You were there. You think I just happened to attack a giant biker for the fun of it?"

"Course not. But a judge might not look at it the same way. See, he comes from a different world, maybe he ain't never been up against a greaser in a parking lot. So he might not understand that it was self-defense."

Bobby relit his joint and took a drag. "And I don't come from my grandfather's world, so I don't have the right to judge him?"

"You got the right," said Mendy gently. "You ever been to Oakland Avenue?"

"Never even heard of it."

"Oakland Avenue's where your grampa started out," said Mendy. "You oughta have a look sometimes."

"He barely even talks to me," said Bobby. "I don't think he's going to take me on a guided tour down memory lane."

"Prob'ly not," said Mendy. "He's not feeling too good these days anyway. But you want me to, I'll do it."

"Why would you want to?" asked Bobby warily.

Mendy picked up Bobby's dirty plate and said, "Same reason I've done everything else my whole life. For the fun of it."

JOHNNY BALDINI STOOD, transfixed, before a bin of fresh asparagus. The sight of a large young man, six foot three, 250 pounds, with a goatee and wire-rim glasses, wearing Bermuda shorts and a rapt expression as he gazed at vegetables was not as unusual at the Livingston farmers market as it would have been in a Grosse Pointe supermarket. The open-air stalls attracted the Johnny Baldinis of three counties, perfectionists willing to drive two hours for extra fresh arugula or individually grown honeydews.

The Livingston market had another, even greater attraction for Johnny Baldini. Once a week he met Annette Tucci there.

Baldini was thirty years old but inexperienced with women. In his life he had only known three well: the grandmother who raised him and taught him to cook in her cramped, aromatic kitchen in Queens; his twelfth-grade teacher, Sister Elizabeth, who recognized his talent and convinced him that cooking was a fit profession for a young man; and now, Annette Tucci.

Annette was Johnny Baldini's patroness, his champion, his confidante, his friend—and his lover. Before they met he had been a virgin, miserably certain that he was homosexual but terrified of physical intimacy with a man. Imperiously, brusquely, Annette had plucked him out of his monkish isolation and plunged him into her sexual broths and gravies. Oddly, Baldini didn't take the affair as proof of his own heterosexuality. He thought of Annette Tucci less as a woman than a mighty, singular, irresistible natural force. He worked for Don Vittorio, but he belonged to Annette.

Baldini had originally come to the Tuccis upon the recommendation of his uncle Mike, who did business in Detroit. On his first evening in the don's kitchen he had prepared one of his finest meals: *rognocini trifolati al vino bianco*—sautéed lamb kidneys in white wine—along with spinach-filled crespelle and an asparagus salad. Don Vittorio had called him from the kitchen and applauded, but Annette had withheld her praise.

The next afternoon she had come to the kitchen. "Today I make dinner," she said. As Johnny watched, she fixed the identical dishes he had prepared the night before. She worked with the fluid, decisive motions of a professional chef, cooking from memory. When she was finished she set the meal before him.

Fearfully Johnny raised a forkful of sautéed lamb to his lips. The job with the Tuccis was important to him, but food was sacred; lying would be out of the question. He chewed tentatively and swallowed.

"Well?" said Annette.

"Magnificent," said Johnny.

"You're an artist," Annette had said. "I just want you to know that you're cooking for an artist."

Now Johnny looked up from his asparagus-induced reverie and saw Annette swaggering toward him on open-backed heels. She wore tight white jeans, a red halter top, and a half smirk that acknowledged the stares of the farmers in the market stalls. She walked up to Johnny and put her arms around his ample paunch, pinching the soft flesh that hung over the waistband of his Bermudas. As usual he was surprised that she came only to his chin; when they were apart he always pictured her as towering above him.

"What have you got?" she asked.

"Fresh sage," said Johnny with a fond look at his shopping basket.

She took his pudgy hand in hers and said, "Let's walk around, see what else looks good."

They took an unhurried turn through the market, stopping now and then to sniff the oregano, ferret out glossy zucchini, inspect the dried wild mushrooms, and nibble at homemade blood sausage. At one of the stalls Annette picked out several eggplants, but when she saw Johnny frown she put them back. The market was the one place she treated him with equality, even deference.

After a while they sat down under an awning to have jelly

donuts and weak American coffee. "Okay," said Annette. "What would you do with wolf?"

"That's a good one," said Johnny. It was a game they played, how to prepare dishes using protected species. "Let's see. Start with a marinade: olive oil, white wine, ground black pepper, sage, rosemary, parsley, and sweet marjoram. Is this an old wolf or a young wolf?"

"A tough old she-wolf," said Annette.

"In that case, I'd marinate for thirty-six hours. Then I'd stew her in her own juice with just a little celery, a bit of sugar, and a clove of garlic, basting with white wine as necessary."

"Sounds delicious," said Annette.

"Add a dash of Romano at the end."

"Why Romano?"

"In honor of Romulus and Remus."

"What if it's in honor of me?" said Annette, sliding her hand down the inside of Johnny's bare thigh. "What would you put in then?"

Johnny blushed.

Annette laughed huskily and darted her hand into Johnny's crotch. "Hey, big boy, is that a *cotechino* in your pocket or are you happy to see me?" she drawled.

Johnny started and looked around wildly; he was afraid, as he always was when she groped him in public, that she'd get them both arrested for indecent behavior. "Why don't we go back to the motel?" he said. A Holiday Inn down the freeway was their regular venue for sex.

"I like it here," said Annette. "Tell me, how would you fix pufferfish?"

"Pufferfish? I've never even seen one. I don't think they're legal in America."

"Of course they're legal," said Annette impatiently. "It's just a fucking fish."

"It can kill you if it's not prepared properly. Something about excretions from the liver."

"Forget that. How would you fix one?"

"Okay," said Johnny. "Let's see. First, is this a young pufferfish or an old pufferfish?"

"Hey, I'm not playing this time. I'm serious. I want you to cook me one."

"I wouldn't dare."

"You wouldn't dare not to," said Annette, glaring at him.

"That's not fair," Johnny said. He was pouting.

Annette had forgotten how petulant he could be when it came to food. "I'm sorry," she said. "I thought you were learning to live dangerously. I guess I've been kidding my-self." She looked away and waited.

"But why take the chance?"

Annette seized Johnny's jowly cheeks and pulled his face close. "You are the greatest goddamn chef in the entire world," she said with passionate conviction. "You want me to believe you can't fix a dish that every short-order cook in Japan can make? That it's beyond you? Is that what you're saying?"

Johnny averted his eyes. "I guess I could find out how to do it."

Annette released him and said, "I knew I could count on you." She took a sip of cold coffee. "Ready to hit the road?"

"Where to?"

"The motel," said Annette. "You're being a good boy, and good boys deserve a prize."

"I thought you didn't want to."

"That's just the way women are," she said. "Flighty as butterflies." She extended her hand, and after a moment's hesitation, Johnny took it. They walked toward the parking lot, Annette striding along with her head high, Johnny shuffling to keep up and sneaking puzzled looks at her from the corner of his eye. He didn't know much about women, but he knew enough to know that Annette Tucci was anything but a butterfly.

"Now, over here's where the Sugar House was," Mendy was saying. "The original hangout of the Purple Gang. Park right up there and I'll show you something."

Bobby, who was driving Tillie's van, gave Mendy an uncertain look. All afternoon the three of them had been cruising Detroit, venturing into neighborhoods full of AME churches and barbecue joints and boarded-up apartment buildings where dark, brooding men sat staring through unfriendly eyes.

They had visited the site of the Collingswood massacre; driven down Twelfth Street, now called Martin Luther King Boulevard—the very epicenter of the 1967 riot—to view the shell of a restaurant where Vittorio had once hosted a dinner for Meyer Lansky and Frank Costello; driven by what had once been Jew Mary's whorehouse off Woodward Avenue ("I was in charge of security there. Your grampa was her best customer") and the now defunct Empress Burlesque. From there they had crossed Woodward into the even more forbidding East Side, to see Joey the Bum's old tavern where Johnny Ray once sang ("He got paid in smack") and the streets where Vittorio Tucci first began to make his name.

Mendy pointed out these places with none of the resentment white Detroiters used in describing their old haunts. Bobby was struck by his good cheer and lack of nostalgia. It was as if the city had never changed, as though Mendy expected to see Cherokee Levine, Frankie "the Farmer" Deloni, or some other member of the old gang emerge from the tumbledown frame houses they passed along the way.

The Sugar House proved to be a vacant store in a row of vacant stores, all dirty cinnamon brick and busted glass. On the corner Bobby spotted two young black men who seemed to be eyeing them with interest.

"Come on, take a look," said Mendy. He opened the door and climbed out, shaking kinks from his arms and legs. Tillie slid out after him, and Bobby reluctantly followed. As he locked his door he could see the black guys gravitating toward them.

"Hey, man," said a tall, cocoa-colored young man who appeared to be the leader. "That's a bad-looking van you got there. Y'all some kind of hippies?" He sounded amused.

Bobby's stomach tightened. As a kid he had tuned in every day to Frantic Ernie D on WJLB, because he loved the

music and because listening to a colored radio station forti-
fied his reputation as the family flake. Over the years he had
mastered the guitar licks and copied the inflections of everybody from Bo Diddley to Jimi Hendrix. But he had met very
few black people in person, and in truth, they frightened him.

"No, man, we're musicians," Bobby said. "You know a cat
named Carver Cleveland? He's in our band."

"Ah, no, I don't believe we know that particular cat," said
the tall guy dryly. He looked at Tillie and his grin widened.
"How you doin' today, princess?"

"It's hot as shit out here, I can tell you that," said Tillie. She
seemed relaxed enough, but Bobby was acutely aware that
they were staring at her. Never had she seemed so white.

"I got some cool drinks up at my crib," said the tall guy.

"Nah, that's all right," said Bobby.

"Didn't nobody ax you," said the short, light-skinned guy
with freckles and a giant mushroom-shaped Afro. He wore a
Black Panther pin on his khaki vest.

Bobby caught a glimpse of Mendy, who had wandered off
in the direction of the vacant building. Before meeting him
Bobby's life had been a model of nonviolence. Now it seemed
like he got into some kind of confrontation every time he left
the house. He seized Tillie's arm and said, "We gotta go."

"Man, y'all just got here," coaxed the tall guy in a mocking
tone.

Mushroomhead took a step toward them. Bobby shifted
his weight, preparing for an assault, just as Mendy came
strolling over with his hands in his pockets. "You guys live
on this street?" he asked.

They looked up, surprised. Mushroomhead said, "What's it to ya? You a cop?"

"Aw. Hey, did you know this street used to be the hangout of the Purples?"

"The what?"

"The Purple Gang. Don't tell me you never heard of the Purple Gang."

"They like them purple people-eaters?" asked the tall guy.

Mendy pointed to the abandoned shops. "That over there was a numbers bank. Pimples Warnick used to run it till one time the number come up seven-one-one and he went broke. Next door was a pawnshop, belonged to a one-armed fence named Seltzer. You could get rid of anything in there. His sister sold smack. Her name was Helen. I heard she's out in California now."

"All that right there in them empty buildings?" asked the tall guy, sounding genuinely curious.

"Sure. You fellas live in a historical neighborhood. Com'ere, lemme show ya." Mendy began walking toward the building. To Bobby's surprise, the black guys followed.

They entered one of the vacant stores, and Mendy said, "We used to lock up guys in here. Fellas somebody had a problem with."

"How you lock 'em up if you ain't got no bars on the windows?" asked the tall guy.

Mendy went to the back of the room and scuffed at the filthy floor with his two-toned shoes. After a moment he said, "Yeah, here it is."

"What?"

"Trapdoor," said Mendy.

"What's down there?" asked Tillie.

Mendy shrugged his shoulders. "The jailhouse. Who's got a knife?"

Mushroomhead whipped out a six-inch gravity blade. He gave Bobby a long look before handing it to Mendy, who flipped it open and ran it along the crease of the trapdoor until he found the lock. There was a click and the door popped up a few inches. Mendy tugged and it swung all the way open, exposing metal stairs that led down to a dark basement.

"Cool," said Tillie. "Let's go take a look."

"That's up to—hey, I'm sorry, I didn't get your name," said Mendy to the tall guy.

"Rudy. This is Delbert," he said, pointing to the mushroomhead.

"You wanna go down, you gotta ask Rudy," Mendy said to Tillie. "This is his turf."

Rudy gave Mendy an appreciative look and said, "Del, run by the A-rab and tell him I need his flashlight. And get some refreshments while you there."

Delbert grumbled but did as he was told. While he was gone, Mendy reminisced about the Jewish and Italian gangs that had once controlled Oakland Avenue.

"Man, those were some cool times," said Rudy. "But let me ask you this—y'all back then, how you think you'd do up against us?"

"We wouldn't stand a chance," said Mendy. "It's just like

sports. Kids today are bigger and stronger. And smarter. You'd wipe up the floor with us."

Delbert returned with a powerful flashlight, a big bag of pork rinds, and two quarts of Jet malt liquor. Rudy took one look and said, "Man, Del, why you bring them rinds?"

"What's wrong with 'em?"

"Don't you know Jews don't eat no swine? Go on back an' get my man Mendy some potato chips. Potato chips all right with you, man?"

"Rudy, man, I ain't no servant," said Delbert.

"Aw, that's all right," said Mendy, taking a handful of rinds. "I don't keep all the rules and regulations."

Rudy flicked on the flashlight. "Let's go have a look at y'all's jailhouse," he said. "Del, you stay up here and make sure don't nobody come along and drop this top back down on us."

The basement was dank and malodorous. Rudy sniffed and said, "Smells like shit."

"It's the kangaroo," said Mendy. "Henry Stutz used to keep a boxing kangaroo down here. We called him Battling Australia. I remember this one time, Australia took on Sonny Rosenberg, who was supposed to be a middleweight fighter, for fifty bucks, and knocked him out. Sonny claimed it was a sneak punch, but Stutz wouldn't give his money back. So Sonny snuck down one day and shot Australia right between the eyes. The place never smelled the same again. It was like a curse."

Rudy flashed his light into the far corners of the basement, but there was nothing there except a few empty tin cans. Bobby lit a match and inspected one of the walls. "Hey," he called, "check this out."

Rudy beamed the light at the wall, which was spotted with graffiti. Some was written in ink, some carved into the plaster.

"Cool," said Tillie. "Gangster hieroglyphics."

"This one say LOUIE KANTER EATS SHIT," said Rudy.

"Jeez, Louie," said Mendy. "He was a nice guy. He got shot in the fifties over a bad debt. His brother Morrie's an Elk, very high up."

"Here's a good one," said Tillie. "LOKSHEN KISS MY ASS. Isn't *lokshen* what you call Italians?"

"It's just a figure of speech in Yiddish," said Mendy. "It means noodles."

"Man, maybe you left a message up there," said Rudy.

"Nah," said Mendy. "Not me."

"How do you know?" said Bobby. "This was like, what? Forty years ago?"

"I know."

"Man's got too much class to be scribbling on walls, that's what he's telling you," said Rudy.

"Nah," said Mendy. "That ain't it. I just don't know how to write."

"At all?" asked Tillie. She had never met anyone who couldn't write.

Mendy shook his head.

"You could learn," she said. "I could teach you."

"Aw," said Mendy. "Tell you the truth, I'm used to it by now."

They came back up blinking into the dim light of the deserted building. "Y'all see some ghosts down there?" asked Delbert sarcastically; he was annoyed at having been left behind.

"Ain't about what was, it's about what *will* be," said Rudy.

"Sure," said Mendy. "Clean it up a little and you got yourself a nice spot. Maybe spray something around, get out the kangaroo."

"Man, you still in the life?" asked Rudy. His tone was entirely respectful now, collegial.

"Nah, I'm retired, got a little diner down by the ballpark, the Bull Pen Deli. You ever go to the ball games?"

"Ain't no brothers go to no ball games," said Delbert in an aggrieved tone. "The Tigers be some prejudiced motherfuckers."

"Drop by anytime," said Mendy to Rudy, "I'll fix you somethin' good to eat. I'm there till three every day but Sunday."

"Yeah, I might will do that," said Rudy. "Talk about what it was like in the days."

To his great surprise, Bobby felt a pang of jealousy. He said, "You dig rhythm and blues, you should come hear us play some night. As my guest. We gig around Detroit sometimes."

"You and your friend, the one got a name sound like a colored high school?" said Delbert.

"Man, what's your problem?" said Bobby. "You've been on my case since we got here."

Delbert stiffened. "I don't like white people," he said.

Delbert and Bobby locked angry stares. After a long, tense moment it was Delbert who looked away. "Shit," he said, "you ain't worth the bother."

On the way home Mendy said, "You and Delbert back there? You done it just right."

"They call it playing the dozens," said Bobby; he knew that from an essay he had read by Eldridge Cleaver.

"You got a nice touch," Mendy said.

And Tillie said, "Yeah. You one bad *lokshen* mother-fucker."

Chapter Nine

ANNETTE HIT O'HARE running, her high heels clicking through the crowded terminal. Directly outside, in a No Standing zone, a black stretch limo was waiting. Her cousin Jo-Jo Niccola was at the wheel. "Hey, cuz," he said. "Welcome to the Windy City."

"Christ, it's good to be home," she said.

They fought traffic all the way from the airport down to Lake Shore Drive, where Jo-Jo wheeled the limo into a well-guarded underground garage. The entire building, fourteen stories, belonged to Tommy Niccola. He lived in the penthouse, and his offices were on the floor below. The rest of the apartments were rented to members of the Family. Anyone trying to get to Tommy the Neck would have to fight his way through twelve floors of Niccolas.

The Neck was waiting at the elevator for his daughter. It had only been a week since her last visit, but when the door opened she flew into his arms. Annette wasn't more than five foot six, but she towered over her father. Niccola's nickname was ironic; he looked like a giant weight had driven his head directly into his massive shoulders.

"How's my honey?" he growled affectionately.

She nuzzled his cheek and said, "Hello, big bear." Then they tightened their embrace and kissed each other on the lips.

"How's your father-in-law?" asked Niccola.

"Six months, tops," said Annette. Like Catello, she had Dr. Florio on her payroll. "He'll be dead by Christmas."

"Your mother died at Christmastime," said Niccola.

"Did she?"

"Yeah. I got stuck with all her presents. Come on, princess, how about a drink?"

"Fix me one. I'll go get changed."

Annette went upstairs to what had been her mother's bedroom and flung open the door of a walk-in closet the size of a squash court. It was full of contraband—furs with the labels removed, counterfeit designer outfits in cleaning bags, stolen silk blouses and cashmere sweaters, boxes of lingerie stacked to shoulder level, and dozens of pairs of Italian pumps arranged by color. Her mother's wardrobe.

Annette stripped down to her bra and panties and inspected herself in the full-length mirror. She was still firm and supple. Better-looking at forty-three, she thought, than she had been at thirty. She slipped into a tight black cocktail dress, cut low in the back. Her mother had been a showgirl who kept her figure. Annette remembered her in this dress.

There was a safe in the closet. Annette spun the combination lock and extracted a blue diamond necklace and matching earrings, a 1934 Cartier diamond watch, and a diamond-and-ruby tennis bracelet. She closed the safe and inspected herself once again. Sexier than her mother, she decided—sexier than her mother at her peak. She touched her neck and wrists with My Sin from the dressing table. It was her father's favorite fragrance.

When Annette came back downstairs she was rewarded with a low whistle of approval. "You're a knockout, princess," said Tommy. "You oughta take some of that stuff back with you to Detroit. The jewels at least."

"They belong here," said Annette. "Besides, in Detroit there's nobody to wear them for."

"Okay, let's talk about Detroit," said Tommy. "You ready?"

Annette nodded.

"What about Catello?"

"I can handle Catello," said Annette. "And Relli, too."

"Relli don't worry me," said Tommy. "But that Catello. . . ." There was no need for him to complete the sentence. Annette knew her father was thinking about Catello's coup de grâce in the war against the Mossi Family.

"Believe me, when the time comes he won't be around to worry you," said Annette. "You got my word on that."

Tommy took a map from his desk and spread it on the

table. It was his master plan, the outlines of a Niccola empire from the Canadian border to the Gulf of Mexico, bounded by Detroit in the East and Kansas City in the West.

"The Center Cut," he had called it the first time he revealed the plan to Annette. "We start out at the top with Chicago, Milwaukee, Minneapolis, and Detroit. Then we drop down like a curtain, all the way to New Orleans and South America. In the middle we got the horses in Kentucky, the booze and the music business in Tennessee, and the oil and the gambling in Louisiana, plus the seaport in New Orleans and the Mississippi River. Hell, we even got Alabama. There must be something down there.

"But the best thing's what we don't got. We got no Five Families to fight with. We got no New York newspapers poking into our business. We got no Washington bureaucrats breathin' down our necks. We got no Mormon politicians stickin' their hands in our pockets like in Vegas. And we ain't got no fucking California." Tommy Niccola distrusted California because the TV programs came on at the wrong times. "What we got is the best part of America, the dumb America, America the stupid. The fuckin' Center Cut. You see it?"

Annette had seen it right away, and she had watched with admiration as her father brought one piece of the center after another into his domain. Now all that was left was Detroit, the gateway to the North and the East. Thanks to her, Detroit was about to fall, the dream was about to become reality.

Tommy ran his stubby hand lovingly over the map and said, "What about Bobby?"

"Bobby's Bobby," she said dismissively.

"Bobby's important," said Tommy. "If he gets the nod from Vittorio, the New York Families will stay out. But if there's a vacuum . . ." His neckless shrug was eloquent.

"I got Vittorio by the short hairs," said Annette. "He'll give it to Bobby."

"I can't stand the kid, but when I croak the whole Center Cut will be his," said Tommy.

"Not for years," said Annette. She let her affection for her father dilute the irritation she felt when he spoke this way. When the time came, her father's successor would not be Bobby. Bobby was weak like his father, Roberto. Worse, he was a Tucci. Annette jabbed a long, laminated fingernail into a scab on her left wrist and watched a tiny bubble of crimson rise to the surface. This is what would entitle her to her father's empire. When the time came. Blood. Niccola blood.

Chapter
Ten

THE DOORBELL RANG twice, and Mendy, dressed in a worn red satin bathrobe, went to answer it. Out of long habit he stood off to the side and called out, "Who's there?"

"It's the feds. This is a raid."

Mendy laughed as he opened the door for Bobby and Tillie, who began serenading him with "Happy Birthday to You."

"Jeez," said Mendy. "How'd you know?"

"Same way we know your address—it's on your driver's license," Bobby said.

"The other night you left your jacket on the chair with your wallet in it," said Tillie.

Mendy said, "You drove all the way down here just to wish me a happy birthday?"

"And to take you out to dinner," said Tillie. "I mean, you don't turn seventy every day and—"

"Mendy, who's there?" called a woman from the other room. Her voice was young-sounding, full of sleep and cigarettes.

"Just some pals stopped by," Mendy called out. "I'll be back in a minute."

Bobby and Tillie looked at each other. "Oops," Tillie said.

"We better split," said Bobby. "Looks like you're already having a birthday party."

Mendy said, "Tell you what. How about we meet around nine at the Riverboat. Mel Tormé's there."

Bobby grinned and said, "Table for four?"

Mendy nodded, then cupped his hand to his mouth in a conspiratorial gesture. "Tonight? Don't say nothin' about this, okay?"

"Don't worry," whispered Tillie. "We won't embarrass her."

A sheepish look came over Mendy's face. "Nah, that ain't it. See, I'll be comin' with a different girl."

WHEN MENDY ARRIVED at the Riverboat with his date, a stylishly dressed woman in her mid-forties named Mildred, Bobby and Tillie were waiting in the parking lot. "Whatcha doin' out here?" he asked.

"They wouldn't let us in," said Tillie. "We're underdressed." Bobby was wearing a pair of faded jeans and a black T-shirt, Tillie a miniskirt and tank top.

"Lemme talk to them," said Mendy.

"It won't do any good," said Bobby. "I already had a few words with the prick at the door."

"A few well-chosen words," giggled Tillie. They were both stoned.

Mendy went inside. Thirty seconds later he was back, along with a stricken-looking maître d'. "What a misunderstanding," he wailed. He ushered them into the club, where waiters were already setting up a table for four in the front.

"They must know you here," said Bobby.

"Everybody knows Mendy," said Mildred. She was a redhead with a big bust and merry blue eyes that darted around the room.

Tillie said, "I bet you slipped him a twenty all folded up in a little square, the way they do it in the movies. Right?"

"Nah," said Mendy. "I just used the magic word."

"'Please'?"

"'Tucci.' Bobby's grampa owns this joint."

"Figures," said Bobby. "Well, that's another use for the family name, getting in to see Mel Tormé."

The manager arrived with a bottle of Moët '69. "Next time, please let me know you're coming," he said to Bobby. "And if there's anything else I can do—"

"No, that's cool," said Bobby. He sensed that people were looking at him.

The band struck up a Tommy Dorsey tune, and Mendy led Mildred to the dance floor, which was filling up with middle-aged men in dark silk suits and women in clinging, sparkly dresses. One bald man danced with an unlit cigar in his mouth. "Can you believe this place?" Tillie giggled.

A man stopped at their table. He had wavy white hair and a giant diamond on his pinky finger. "Sam Zaramis," he said in a gravelly voice. "Me and your grampa go back."

"Nice to meet you," said Bobby.

"Pleasure's all mine. Be sure an' remember me to your grampa. Sam Zaramis." He made an awkward half bow and walked away.

No sooner had Zaramis left than another man came up. He, too, was in late middle age. He, too, wore a pinky ring. "Allie Alkarian," he said, shaking Bobby's hand. "Me and your dad, Roberto, were close, God rest his soul. Maybe he mentioned me sometime?"

Bobby shook his head. "Sorry—"

"Hey, I just wanted to come by and pay my respects," Alkarian said. "Enjoy the show."

"And to think, I loved you even before I found out you were royalty," said Tillie.

"Let's dance," said Bobby.

"To this? No way. You'll kill my feet."

"You dance with Mendy and I'll take Mildred. She looks like she knows how to lead."

They danced for a while, and then Mel Tormé came on. All through the show waiters kept refreshing their drinks. When the first set ended, Mildred rose and said to Tillie, "Let's go powder our noses."

"Okay," Tillie said. "But I have to piss first."

As they walked away Bobby said, "Nice lady."

"Sure. She's tops."

"Good thing you warned us about not mentioning this afternoon."

Mendy hitched his shoulders and widened his eyes, like a mischievous kid. "Yeah, that wouldn't have been too good."

"Mildred's the jealous type, huh?"

"Aw, it's not that," said Mendy. "But see, that girl I was with today? That was her daughter."

"Whose daughter?"

"Mildred's."

Bobby threw his head back and laughed. "You're screwing Mildred's daughter?"

"It's not a serious thing."

"How old is she? If you don't mind my asking?"

"Karen? She's, ah, about twenty-five, twenty-six. Somewhere in there."

Bobby shook his head. "Un-fucking-believable," he said.

"Prob'ly you shouldn't mention it to Tillie," said Mendy. "It's not the kind of thing a guy should tell a broad. Let's just keep it between us."

"Okay," said Bobby. He couldn't wait to tell Tillie.

"Good. Hey, look who's here!" Bobby turned and saw a man approaching. He was younger than the guys who had come over before, around forty, with less flesh on his face. Mendy introduced him as Jackie Glass. When he shook Bobby's hand his grip was strong. Bobby noticed that he wasn't wearing a pinky ring.

"You're Roberto's kid," said Glass, sizing Bobby up with a frank, almost clinical stare.

Bobby nodded; he didn't like the vulpine look on the man's face. "You were a great pal of my dad's, right?"

"You got me mixed up with somebody," said Jackie. "Me and him did a little business from time to time, but that's about it."

"Oh."

"You got the place buzzing," Jackie said. "The two of you."

"It's my birthday," said Mendy. "Bobby and his girl are helping me celebrate."

"Many happy returns," said Jackie. "Listen, Bobby, this isn't a good place to talk, but I got a proposition the Tuccis might be interested in. I was going to speak to the don direct, but maybe you'd like to take it to him. You want, we could get together later and discuss it."

Bobby felt light-headed from the champagne and grass. What the fuck, he thought. "What kind of proposition?"

Jackie Glass shot a look at Mendy, who responded with an affirmative blink. "Without getting into the details, a million bucks in cash will net you out three within thirty days."

"How?"

"It's in the nature of an international financial transaction," said Glass.

"Drugs?"

Glass nodded. "Yeah."

"Grass? Or coke?"

"The former."

"Good shit?"

"Primo," said Glass.

"Cool," said Bobby. "Tell you what. You score really good shit, I'll take a key. How's that?"

Glass looked at Mendy and said, "I make a mistake here?"

Mendy shrugged.

"How about it, Bobby? I make a mistake talking to you?"

"Look, Mr. Glass," said Bobby, "I don't make drug deals with strangers in nightclubs. The only reason I'm buying the key off you is because you're a friend of Mendy's."

Glass stood. "We never had this conversation," he said.

"Sure, no problem," Bobby said. "It's been nice not meeting you."

After the second show, Bobby and Tillie headed back to Ann Arbor, leaving Mendy and Mildred with a table full of complimentary drinks. On the way Bobby recounted his conversation with Jackie Glass. "While he was talking I sat there thinking—two generations of Tuccis have spent their lives making deals with assholes like him."

"Yeah, and for what?" said Tillie. "A paltry couple hundred million dollars."

He laughed. "Think I blew it?"

"Well, it doesn't sound like we're gonna get that key."

"Know what Mendy said? He said, 'I never like a fella who's too big to sell retail.' "

"Words to live by," said Tillie. "You're not going to believe what Mildred told me."

"You're not going to believe what *Mendy* told *me*," Bobby

said. "You know that girl at his place today? Guess who she was."

"Okay. I guess it was Mildred's daughter."

"How do you know?" asked Bobby.

"Mildred told me when we were powdering our noses. She said not to let on to Mendy that she knows."

"Poor Mendy," said Bobby. "Busted. Mildred's not pissed?"

"She didn't seem to be," said Tillie. "Of course she wouldn't. Under the circumstances."

"What circumstances?"

"Did Mendy happen to mention how he met her?"

"Mildred? No. How?" Her tone made him grin.

"At his wedding."

"His wedding?"

"Yep," said Tillie. She began to giggle. "He's married. To Mildred's aunt."

Chapter Eleven

ALBERTO RELLI DRESSED carefully for his date with Annette Tucci. He considered himself a handsome man in a rough-hewn way, despite the fact that his prominent nose and his mouth bent slightly rightward, the result of a childhood illness. When he was young he patterned himself on Tony Curtis, until he found out that Tony's real name was Schwartz. After that he chose Dean Martin for his model. He wore his hair like Dino's—in a ducktail with a little curl up front—favored cashmere sport jackets, and rarely put on a tie. It was a look, he felt, that worked for him, a fact attested to by his many romantic conquests.

Relli's wife was a blowsy peroxide blonde named Tina, the daughter of a small-time loan shark he had married before his rise to prominence. They lived with their three teenaged children in Grosse Pointe Woods, a ritzy suburb not too far from the don's mansion. Relli kept his girlfriend, a tattooed French-Canadian lap dancer called Mitzy, in an apartment downtown, just across the river from the row of strip clubs known as the Windsor ballet. He also had a longtime mistress, a cokehead named Sue, who taught seventh-grade history in Royal Oak. And lately he had rented an apartment near the airport for a Northwest stew with a dirty mind who spent weekends in Detroit. Relli was well pleased by these arrangements. Unlike Luigi Catello, who depended on pickups because he was too cheap to support his women, Alberto Relli was rarely more than ten miles away from a homemade blow job.

Tonight he was planning to add Annette Tucci to his stable. She would be a sweet acquisition. When Roberto croaked, he had made some advances, which she had shot down in a snooty way. But now, with the don dying and power about to shift, Annette had become friendly. That's why she had invited him to dinner at her big house on Lake St. Clair. She was a smart broad, Annette. She knew how things were headed.

When he thought about Luigi Catello he had to laugh. Catello, who had said that Relli needed him to be his eyes. It was Catello who was in the dark, Catello who knew nothing about the don's plans for the Family. Plans that would put Relli at the top.

It crossed his mind that maybe Annette knew something. Not that the don would tell her, but her old man had friends on the National Commission. All the better, he decided. Just thinking about the contract he had been given by Don Vittorio gave Alberto a massive hard-on. Annette was the kind of broad who would respond to that, no question.

A gnocchi like Catello would be scared shit of Annette. But Relli wasn't scared of broads, and he wasn't worried about Tommy the Neck making a move on Detroit. After he carried out the contract, Relli would be named Tucci's successor—he had the old man's word on that—and the Commission would have no choice but to ratify it. Combine that with the army he could put on the street, and he was in an unassailable position.

Relli couldn't believe his luck. Until yesterday he had been a hammer—tough, feared, respected, but no different from a dozen top enforcers around the country. But now he was destined to become not only a boss but a legend. Not since the hit on Bugsy Siegel in L.A. had there been such a plum assignment for a man in his profession. By the end of the summer he would be known to the members of the National Commission and a few select insiders as Don Alberto Relli—boss of Detroit, the man who whacked Jimmy Hoffa.

After Relli took over the Family, Luigi Catello would be as dispensable as a used razor blade. Annette was another story. She was royalty twice over, a Niccola and a Tucci. An alliance with her would be a class move. Plus the expansion thing could work both ways; with the Princess of Chicago at his side, he might be able to stick a toe in the Windy City.

Relli paused for a moment and thought about his wife. Divorce was out of the question, but accidents happened. On the other hand, Annette wasn't the kind of broad who would insist on a wedding ring.

Relli took a fond last look at the mirror, pulled in his stomach, and gave himself a loopy Dean Martin grin. There were butterflies in his belly when he thought about Annette. People said he was a hard guy. Nobody knew how romantic he really was inside.

ANNETTE CAME TO the door on five-inch heels and a cloud of My Sin. Her black silk dress clung to her body; around her neck she wore a pearl choker that made her look like a sexy nun. It was an outfit Catholic men usually found irresistible, and she saw from his expression that Alberto Relli was not an exception. Relli's reputation as a ladies' man amused her. She regarded him and his sunlamp tan, three-hundred-dollar Italian loafers, Brylcreem pompadour, and Rat Pack smirk as not much more of a challenge than Johnny Baldini.

Annette led Relli to a sunporch that overlooked the lake. The room was lit with candles, the table set for two; Mantovani murmured in the background. There was a steaming pot on the table. Relli sniffed and said, "Something smells terrific."

"Greathead stuffed with crab and shrimp," said Annette. "Sautéed in butter with thyme and a little lemon. It's my own recipe."

"Greathead, that's a fish?"

"I hope you like fish."

"Absolutely," said Relli. "Especially if it's cooked by you."

During dinner they exchanged Family gossip as Relli devoured his meal, washing it down with two bottles of chilled white wine. Then Annette brought in tiramisu and a bottle of Hennessy VO. "Let's have our dessert in the living room," she said. "It's cozier."

Relli sank into the large white couch with a satisfied grunt. Annette handed him a porcelain hash pipe. Relli grinned; things were going just right. He took a hit, held the smoke, and then expelled it with a violent cough.

"You okay?" she asked.

"Strong shit. Very nice."

Annette took the pipe and said, "I laced it with a little opium."

Relli stretched on the couch, letting his arm fall over Annette's shoulder. "Great food, great dope, great looks, you got the whole package," he said expansively. "How come you and me never got together before this?"

"We're not together yet," said Annette. "I'm still thinking about it."

"You never thought I was in your league," said Relli.

"You weren't."

"But I am now."

"Maybe."

"Fuckin' A," said Relli. He took another hit of the hashish and closed his eyes as he exhaled. When he opened them it seemed to him that Annette was looming very close and very large. "Just wait a few more weeks, you'll see what league I'm in," he said.

"What's then?"

"That's when things break big for me," said Relli. He took another hit off the pipe and washed it down with some Hennessy.

"Oh?"

"You don't know?"

She shook her head. Relli began to say something, reconsidered, and immediately forgot what it was. After a silence that could have been seconds or minutes long, Annette stirred and said, "Let's go down to the rumpus room and shoot some pool."

Relli's stoned brain recognized this as a bad idea. It was dark, the couch was soft, and he could feel the warmth of Annette's body. Eight-ball would definitely break the mood. He pulled her toward him and said, "I'm gonna be the next don. After I do my thing."

"What thing?"

More time passed and Relli said, "Numb Hoffa."

"Jimmy Hoffa?"

"He's getting whacked," said Relli.

"Right," said Annette. "They've been whacking out Jimmy Hoffa since my first communion."

"Except this time it's for real," said Relli. "The Commission gave the green light. Carmine Patti was out here the other day setting it up with the don."

Annette fired up another bowl of hashish, took a hit, and

passed it to Relli. "The don's a friend of Hoffa's," she said. "He's been to the house a dozen times."

"The don's hands are tied. Hoffa's pissed off 'cause he can't get his union back. He's threatening to rat out everybody. Friendship don't figure into it."

Annette said nothing. The silence grew heavy, and Relli closed his eyes and drifted off. When he opened them, she was standing before him, naked except for the choker and the heels. He stared at her with admiration. "You're a beautiful broad, you know that?" he slurred.

"I'm gonna do something for you," she said, lowering her nude body onto his lap. "Something you're really going to like." She licked his ear. "And then, I'm gonna ask you to do something for me."

"I don't give head," he mumbled.

She ran her hand down his thigh and said, "That's all right, baby, I don't need your head. All I want is a little help."

"Anything," said Relli. He was panting now.

Annette darted her tongue into his thick, hairy ear. "Be a father to Bobby," she whispered.

"Sure, babe," gasped Relli. At that moment he had no idea who Bobby might be. Then, from the deep recesses of his hash-fried brain came the realization that she was talking about her son. Broads are all alike, he thought; no matter how hot they act, they're still just mothers at heart.

Chapter Twelve

TILLIE INVITED MENDY to a Fourth of July picnic at her family's cottage on Cass Lake. "Bring a date," she told him on the phone.

"Nah, I'll come stag," he said. "You never know when you're gonna get lucky at the beach." But when he arrived he wasn't alone. Bobby, who was out in the yard stoking up the barbecue pit, saw Mendy's old Plymouth pull in the driveway, followed by a black limousine. Carlo Seluchi was at the wheel, and in the back, looking small, sat Don Vittorio Tucci. Bobby blinked in disbelief. In his entire life he had never seen his grandfather outside the house.

Bobby darted into the kitchen where Tillie and her mother were making potato salad. "Mendy's here," he said excitedly. "And you're not going to believe who else."

Tillie said, "Don't tell me he brought one of his flankens with him. That's what he calls women sometimes, flanken; it's the Yiddish word for beef," she explained to her mother.

"Oh," said Ann Tillman. She found the idea of having a retired gangster to lunch pleasantly confusing.

"It's my grandfather," said Bobby.

"Your grandfather?" said Tillie. "Which one?"

"Vittorio," said Bobby. "He's right out there."

"How nice," said Ann Tillman. She turned to the cook, a dour Mexican woman who had been shelling corn. "Lu, will you finish up in here? I want to greet our guests." Without waiting for an answer, she went banging into the yard. "Welcome," she called. "I'm so glad you could come."

Mendy doffed his straw fedora, gave Ann Tillman a smiling once-over, and said, "Now I see where Tillie gets her good looks. Meet Bobby's grampa, Don Vittorio Tucci."

"Nice to meet you, Don," said Ann. The old man nodded formally, but Bobby thought he saw his lips twitch in amusement. If so, it was another first; he could never recall his grandfather smiling before.

"I'm so sorry my husband, Sandy, isn't here," Ann said. "He's in Switzerland on business. Actually I think you might know him, Don. At least he seems to know you. Sandy Tillman? International Bank and Trust?"

Tucci shook his head noncommittally. He was dressed in a black silk suit that hung off his shrunken shoulders, a gleaming white shirt three sizes too big for his neck, and a subdued amber tie. His black wing tips glistened in the July sun, and there were beads of sweat on his forehead.

"If you'd like to go sailing before lunch I'd love to take you out," said Ann. "We have some beach clothes here that should fit."

"You go," said Tucci. "I wanna stay here and talk to Bobby for a while."

"How about it, Mendy?" said Ann brightly. "Are you game?"

"I doubt if Mendy sails, Mom," said Tillie.

"Are you kidding? Back during Pro'bition I spent half my time on boats. I even got shot once by the Coast Guard."

"Where?" asked Tillie.

Mendy blushed. "In the *tochis.* The hind end. We was crossing over from Canada with a shipment of booze. I figure one of the other outfits paid the Guard to take a few potshots, try to scare us off."

Ann Tillman was incredulous. "They bribed the Coast Guard?"

Mendy shrugged and said, "You'd be surprised who you can bribe."

Tillie took Mendy by the arm and started toward the dock. Bobby watched them go with anxiety. He had never before had a one-on-one conversation with his grandfather.

"Nice-looking girl," said Tucci. "You planning to get married to her?"

"I dunno," said Bobby. Seeing his grandfather waxy in the sun, dressed up like his own corpse, gave Bobby the creeps.

"Her old man's the Michigan bagman for the Republican National Committee," Tucci said. "He's lucky he didn't go to jail with the rest of them Nixon guys."

"I thought you said you didn't know him."

"I know him," said Tucci. There was a long silence, and then he said, "You know why I told you that?"

Bobby shook his head.

"Because if you *do* marry her, somebody might think you're moving up in the world, a Tucci marrying a Tillman. So I want you to know her father's a bum. Her grandfather was a bum too. He owned the worst slums on the East Side."

"Whereas the Tuccis are paragons of civic virtue," said Bobby.

"This might be my last day outside," said Tucci mildly. "Do me a favor, don't fuck it up."

"Sorry," said Bobby. He wasn't sure if he meant it or not. "So you came out here to do what? Commune with nature?"

"I came out to talk," Vittorio said. "There's a couple things we need to get cleared up before I croak—"

HEY, I GOT IT," said Mendy. Tillie and Ann were already on board, but he had lagged behind, his eyes shut in concentration. Now they popped open and he snapped his fingers. "The Roostertail. You used to dance down there, right?"

"I don't know what you mean," said Ann.

"There was a dancer looked just like you in the line at the Roostertail, back in, oh, '49, '50, around in there. I bet that was you."

Tillie laughed. "My mother the chorus girl. I can just picture it."

Ann smiled at Mendy and said, "I'm afraid you've got the wrong girl. I'm embarrassed to tell you this, but I was away at finishing school."

"Well, you got your money's worth," said Mendy approvingly. "Besides, now that I think about it, you're a lot better-looking than her. She didn't have your creamy skin."

"Watch out for Mendy, Mom," said Tillie playfully. "He's got girlfriends all over the place. I hear he's even got a wife stashed away somewhere."

"Hey, how'd you know about her?"

"Mildred. So, are you really married?"

Mendy shrugged. "I might be. I'm not sure."

"You must know if you're married," said Ann, in the same tone she'd used about the Coast Guard.

"I was," Mendy said, "but when I went in the joint she took off for Vegas and we didn't keep in touch. She might have got a divorce, I dunno."

"You got in a little trouble and she split," said Tillie. "Very nice."

"Aw," said Mendy. "I went up for six years. That's an awful long stretch for a hard charger like Dixie."

Tillie laughed. "Dixie Pearlstein?"

"Nah, she went by Dixie Dixx. Miss Dixie Dixx and her bag of Trixx. That was her stage moniker. Her real name was Dotty Kless." A sweet smile crept onto Mendy's lips. "Jeez, she had some frame," he said. "I hope she's doin' good, wherever she is."

I'M HAPPY YOU and Mendy are buddies," said Vittorio. "Mendy's a good man."

"The grandfather I never had," said Bobby, making no effort to hide the sarcasm. He had decided to give Vittorio Tucci exactly what the old man had given him for the past twenty-one years—nothing.

A sudden chill made Tucci shiver—eighty-five degrees out and his bones were cold. "You wanna know why I wasn't palsy-walsy with you? Fine. First of all, your old man didn't want me around you. He thought I'd fuck you up."

"Bullshit," said Bobby. "My father worshipped you. He pissed away his whole life working for you."

"He worked for me, yeah, 'cause he didn't know how to do anything else. Maybe that was my fault, but that's how we raised our kids back then. But if you think he worshipped me, you're full of shit. In the beginning, yeah, but not later. He said I made a deal with the devil."

"Did you?"

Tucci shrugged. "I'll find out soon enough. Anyway, that's one of the reasons. Another one is your mother. She's an evil bitch."

"Man, once you get started you don't beat around the bush," said Bobby.

"I hate her no-neck old man, and I hate her. After Roberto died, having you around meant seeing her, and it wasn't worth it."

"Thanks."

"That's the other thing," said Tucci. "That snotty la-di-da way you've got of talking, it rubs me the wrong way. Like you think you're so much better than me. Sometimes I see the look on your face when I talk, like my words are farts, stinkin' up the place."

"Maybe that's because you talk like a Hollywood gangster," said Bobby. He had been stung by his grandfather's bluntness. "You grew up in Detroit, not the Bowery."

"You were *born* in Detroit, and you still talk like fuckin' Little Lord Fauntleroy," said Tucci.

"It wasn't my idea to send me away to prep school," said Bobby hotly. "I was just a little kid—"

"Your old lady sent you away 'cause she didn't want you around, and Roberto was too much of a sissy to stand up to her. I figured you for a weak sister like your father, but maybe I got you wrong. Mendy says that underneath the long hair and the faggy accent you're a tough kid. I hope he's right, 'cause you're gonna need to be."

Bobby gave his grandfather a quizzical look. "Is it possible you just made me an apology?"

Don Vittorio grunted. "Yeah, maybe," he said. "It's a little late, but okay. I'm sorry I didn't pay you more attention."

"Thanks," said Bobby. This time he meant it.

"Only I didn't come out here to make an apology," said Don Vittorio. He leaned over and, with surprising strength, drew his grandson so close Bobby could smell the olive oil and garlic oozing from the old man's pores. "I came to give you a warning."

I WONDER IF IT would be rude to ask you a question," said Ann. She and Mendy were sitting in the rear of the sailboat as Tillie steered in the hot July breeze. The women had stripped down to their bathing suits. Mendy had removed his sport jacket and rolled up the sleeves of his white-on-white shirt, but he kept his fedora planted firmly on his head. "Were you really a member of the Purple Gang? You don't have to tell me if you don't want to, but—"

"That's okay," said Mendy. "We didn't have no official memberships like the *lokshen* do, but sure, I bummed around with the Purples."

"You'll think this is awfully funny, but when I was little our nanny used to tell us, 'Eat your supper or the Purple Gang will come and steal it.'"

"No kiddin'?"

"Truly," said Ann. "May I ask you another question? Why were you sent to prison?"

"Which time?"

"When your wife left you."

"A jewel heist."

Ann's blue eyes widened. "That sounds so romantic. Like David Niven on the French Riviera."

"This one took place in the railroad station downtown," said Mendy. "December of 1950. I was running an after-hours joint off Six Mile Road at the time—not a classy spot, but it made a nice dollar and I was keeping my nose clean. Then one day I get a call from Vittorio. He says a rabbi named Farber who works in the diamond business is coming to town with a satchel full of stones. At first I didn't want any part of it. I mean, I'm forty-five years old at the time, I got a wife, and I don't wanna go back to the joint. But then I started thinking about it, and I decided what the hell."

"How much money was involved?" asked Ann in a hushed voice.

"Half a million bucks," said Mendy. "But it wasn't the dough. I was bored. I did it for the thrill. Only it didn't turn out so good."

"What happened?"

"When Farber come off the train I grabbed him and said, in Yiddish, 'We need another Jew for a *minyan*'—that's like a quorum. At first he didn't wanna do it but I told him this guy's mother just died a few weeks ago and he's gotta say the prayer for the dead only his train leaves for Chicago in twenty minutes. Farber's a rabbi, he can't say no to that. I bring him over to where I've got a few knock-around guys I hired for ten bucks each. Soon as they see us they start *davening*—that means praying. What's Farber gonna do? He starts in too, holding his satchel against his chest with both hands. After a while he forgets himself and puts the bag down between his feet. I got this kid, Shelly the Sneak, over in the corner of the station in a pair of Keds. I slip him the high sign and he comes running up and snatches the bag. Farber tries to take off after him, but I give him the trip. By the time he's back on his feet, Shelly's out the door."

"Poor man," said Ann. "I suppose the diamonds were in-sured, though."

"Shelly runs out of the station and bunks right into a cop. All he hadda do was pretend he's rushin' to catch a cab. In-stead he throws up his hands and says, 'Don't shoot, it was all Mendy's idea.'

"Oh," said Ann. "How awful."

"Aw, I can't blame Shelly," said Mendy. "He was just a kid, he panicked. I shoulda planned the escape better. It woulda saved me six years."

"Six years seems like a very long time for a robbery," said Ann. "I'm no expert, but you weren't even armed."

"I had a little bad luck on that," Mendy said. "I got a Jew-ish judge."

Ann laughed uncertainly and said, "Is anyone else ready for lunch?" She was hungry, and she felt like a gin-and-tonic. Mendy Pearlstein was old enough to be her father, but to her great surprise she found him exciting. There was something about the way he looked at her that made her glad that her husband was in Switzerland.

VITTORIO TUCCI SAT with Bobby on the Tillmans' screened porch and watched the little sailboat bob on the water. The sight of it sent a wave of nausea through him. He wanted to lie down with a wet towel on his head, but he wasn't finished with Bobby yet. He summoned the will to keep his voice strong and said, "In a few weeks, things are gonna pop around here. Maybe I'll be dead by then, but it don't matter, they're gonna pop with or without me. And you're gonna be in the middle. People are gonna come to you—your mother and her old man, Catello, Relli, the New York Families, and I dunno who else. They're gonna promise you big money, tell you about your responsibilities, warn you about each other. You understand what I'm sayin'?"

"Why would anyone bother with me?" asked Bobby. "They know I've got nothing to do with the Family."

Don Vittorio paused, thinking about Maria Mossi. There were certain things the kid didn't need to be told. "You're the last Tucci," he said. "You got the name, and whoever gets you on their side has the strongest claim. In a battle royale the name's gonna carry weight. Now do you understand?"

Bobby nodded. Tucci said, "These people who come to you? Don't trust any of them. Especially not your mother. This time when she's done with you, you ain't goin' to no prep school. The only guy you can rely on is Mendy. He's an experienced man, and he's got your interests at heart."

"That's why you put us together?"

"Yeah, mostly." A spasm of coughing shook Don Vittorio's body and filled his eyes with tears. Bobby said, "Grampa, are you all right?"

"Fine," said Don Vittorio. "You lean on Mendy the Pearl, but don't let him decide for you. He ain't the smartest guy in the world, and he ain't no Tucci. You decide for yourself. Got it?" He reached into the pocket of his suit coat and took out an envelope. "This is for you."

"What is it?

"Swiss bank-account numbers and the name of a guy in Zurich. The dough in the accounts is yours. Forty million bucks."

"Holy shit," said Bobby. "I never knew you had that much."

Don Vittorio's ravaged eyes flashed. "Kid, forty million ain't even the interest on what I got," he said. "But it's all *you* get. The legit businesses go to the Roberto Tucci Foundation. I got a crooked judge setting it up. As far as the action goes, just make sure you stay out of the line of fire."

Bobby fingered the envelope. "Does Mendy know about this?"

"All but the Swiss accounts," said Don Vittorio. "Tell him if you want, he won't give a shit. He don't care about money. Okay, that's what I came to say. Do me a favor, gimme a hand back to the car."

Bobby took his grandfather's arm and walked with him to the limo. "I wish we would have had this talk a long time ago," said Bobby.

"Sure, forty million bucks," said Don Vittorio.

"That's not what I meant."

"What, you think you would have discovered that I'm really some lovable old geezer? Bullshit. I'm just who you always thought I was. The money I'm leaving you is blood money. The only reason you're getting it is because I got nobody else to give it to. Besides, I want a favor."

"What favor?"

"I want you to come to my funeral with Mendy," he said, grimacing as he lowered his body into the limo. Perched in the plush backseat he looked tiny and pecked-at. "He's gonna need a friend that day. He'll be the only guy there who misses me."

Bobby wanted to tell his grandfather that it wasn't true, that he'd miss him. Instead he took the envelope from his pocket and said, "I promise. And thanks for this."

"That's okay, kid," said Don Vittorio, rolling up the window. "I hope you live long enough to spend it."

Chapter Thirteen

MENDY WAS BEHIND the counter kibbitzing with a downtown defense attorney and a bail bondsman when Rudy walked in. Mendy looked up and grinned. "My *landsman* from Oakland Avenue."

Rudy took a seat at the counter, gave the white men a friendly nod, and said to Mendy, "You get a free minute, I got something to show you."

"Sure," said Mendy.

"Over on Oakland."

"I finish in about an hour," Mendy said. "Stick around, have some lunch. I got nice brisket."

"Brisket be fine," said Rudy. He gestured to the kitchen. "You got any produce back there? Tomatoes, lettuce, shit like that?"

"You want a salad?"

Rudy shook his head. "You got some extra, I'd like to carry it over there with us," he said. "It don't have to be fresh, you know what I mean?"

Mendy shrugged. All his life he had heard strange requests from guys like Rudy. "Finish your lunch, you can go back in the kitchen and take what you want," he said. "Don't worry, I got plenty."

At three-thirty, when Mendy closed the diner, the vegetables were already loaded in the trunk of Rudy's car. "You wanna ride with me?" Rudy asked.

"Nah, I'll follow ya," Mendy said. "That way you won't have to bring me back."

"Hey, that's cool, I don't mind."

"Aw, you're a young guy, you got better things to do with your time," Mendy said, climbing into his Plymouth.

It took fifteen minutes to reach Oakland Avenue. They parked and Rudy led Mendy toward the row of stores that had once belonged to the Purple Gang. "Check this out," he said proudly.

Mendy whistled and said, "Hey, not bad." The dirty cinnamon brick had been scrubbed clean, new plate-glass windows protected by iron grillwork installed, and there was a handsome wood door. Over it, in Old English lettering, were the words: DETROIT EAST SIDE PURPLE HEART ASSOCIATION. Rudy read them to Mendy.

"This be the place where folks with a Purple Heart from the war against American racism can retreat for a healing hand," he said. "I came up with that shit for the grant people at the Ford Foundation. What you think?"

"Sounds good," said Mendy. "How much they give you?"

"Hundred thousand to start," said Rudy proudly.

"Nice scam," said Mendy. "Very nice."

"Thanks," Rudy said. "But you know what? I really chose that name in y'all's honor. The purple part. Since you the one pulled my coat to the fact that this is a historical spot and all."

"Jeez, that's a hell of a gesture," said Mendy. "Y'know, there's a few of the boys still around. I'd like to bring 'em by sometime. They'd be touched."

"That'd be real nice," said Rudy. He opened the front door with a key and said, "Come on in. I got another surprise for you. Something you gonna appreciate."

Once again Mendy whistled. The room was freshly painted and spotlessly clean. Delbert, a black beret perched on his mushroom Afro, sat at a metal desk reading a copy of *Jet.* When he saw Mendy he scowled.

"Don't pay Delbert no mind," said Rudy easily. "He's just sore cause he got an ass-whuppin'."

"I hope you got in a few licks at least," Mendy said to him.

Delbert exhaled a long "shit" and returned to his magazine. Rudy went to the trapdoor, popped it open, and said, "Hey, looka here."

Mendy heard loud thumping noises. "What's that?" he asked, peering down into the dark basement. Rudy flashed a light, and Mendy blinked in amazement. He was looking at a seven-foot kangaroo.

"Just like the one y'all had," said Rudy. "I call him Ali, 'cause he's so quick and bad."

"Jeez," said Mendy. "He's a beauty. Where'd you get him?"

"Detroit Zoo," said Rudy. "Me and Delbert picked him up last night. That's who kicked Del's ass, the kangaroo. Ain't that right, Del?"

"Shit."

Mendy started chuckling. "What're they, givin' away kangaroos out there?"

"All you need's a big van and a Uzi, the man out there give you any damn animal you want," said Rudy. He flipped Delbert his keys. "Del, man, I got a trunk full of green groceries. Go on out and fetch Ali his dinner."

"That kangaroo put another hand on me, I'm gonna shoot him in his motherfuckin' ass," grumbled Delbert, picking up the keys.

Rudy shut the trapdoor and led Mendy to a small room in the back. A sign on the door said, EXECUTIVE OUTREACH DIRECTOR. "This is my office," he said. He produced a bottle of Chivas and said, "Care for a taste?"

"Sure." Mendy raised his glass in a silent toast, tossed down the whiskey, and smacked his lips. "This is a hell of a setup you got here."

"Yeah," Rudy said softly. "You know what I told you out there? That I picked our name as a tribute to you? I meant it, man. You one inspiring old dude."

"Aw," said Mendy.

"I ain't never met no real gangster before. You ever know Al Capone?"

"Nah, I never met him," said Mendy. "I knew a cousin of his, though. Ralph."

"Ralph Capone?"

"Yeah. He was a cat burglar, worked a lot around Battle Creek, Grand Rapids, up in there. Good guy."

"Uh-huh," said Rudy. He seemed disappointed. "How about er, ah, Dillinger?"

Mendy shook his head. "I think you got the wrong idea about me," he said. "I was just a knock-around guy, like Delbert out there. I banged heads, I hauled booze, I did a few stickups, some loan-sharking. Once I ran a crap game at a hotel downtown. Another time I was the security guy for a whorehouse. I made a good living, I'm not complaining. But I was never big-time."

"Yeah, but you was there," said Rudy. "You seen it all. Fine foxes selling Cuban cigars in nightclubs, private casinos where you gotta say, 'Joe sent me,' all that shit from the movies."

"Oh, sure, I seen it," said Mendy.

"Y'all had style," said Rudy. "Capone and Lucky Luciano and them. They didn't play this Superfly bullshit we got today."

Mendy said, "I dunno. Seems pretty much the same to me. When you come right down to it, it's still tough kids tryin' to make a crooked buck. Take you. You woulda fit right in with the Purples, except you're a colored guy. We didn't have no integrated mobs back then."

"Say I would have fit right in?"

"Sure, I seen it the first time we met," said Mendy. He gazed around the refurbished headquarters. "Look what you done here, it's beautiful. You're usin' your head, ripping off the Fords for a hundred grand. Hell, all we ever got out of 'em was twenty bucks a day for strike-breaking." Mendy looked at his watch. "Hey, I gotta scoot, I got a hot date with a banker's wife and I need a manicure."

Rudy said, "Man, how old are you?"

"Just turned seventy."

"And you still chasin' pussy," said Rudy with admiration. "You my role model, man. You ever need anything from the New Breed Purples, you let me know."

"I'll keep it in mind," said Mendy.

On the way out they ran into Delbert, whose mood had brightened considerably. "You feed Ali?" asked Rudy.

"Yeah," Delbert said with a satisfied laugh. "I threw the food down there, and then when he come to get it I pissed on his got-damned head. Showed that motherfucker who's boss."

"You the boss of a kangaroo," Rudy said dryly.

"Damn right."

Rudy turned to Mendy and said, "This kangaroo-pissing motherfucker ain't gonna make it to thirty. That's why you an inspiration, man. You may not be no Al Capone, but you got over. Seventy motherfuckin' years old and you still alive."

So, Bobby, your mom tells me you're a musician," said
Alberto Relli. "Whaddya play? Disco?"

Bobby looked around his mother's living room. Even Annette would have been a welcome diversion, but she had
dumped them together and gone into the kitchen, where she
and Johnny Baldini were preparing dinner. "Mostly rhythm
and blues," he said. "Soul music."

"Sammy Davis, Jr., like that?"

"Not exactly." Alberto Relli was a man Bobby had known
very slightly for the better part of his life. He didn't know
much about him, but he knew enough not to get smart.
"Bobby Blue Bland? Hank Ballard? Etta James?"

Relli shook his head.

"It's sort of like Motown."

"Motown," Relli said. There was a name he knew. In Detroit it was widely rumored that the Tucci Family had been behind Berry Gordy's sudden decision to relocate his company to California. Even Bobby had heard those stories. "That record business is a tough business. Before you sign any papers you talk to me."

"I'm not planning to make a career of it," said Bobby. "But thanks for the offer."

There was a long silence, and then Relli said, "Me and your mom have gotten pretty close lately. She mention that?"

Bobby shook his head.

"She's a great girl, your mom. Maybe that sounds funny to you, somebody calling her a girl, but that's how she seems to me. Understand what I'm saying?"

Bobby nodded, not trusting his voice.

"I mean it as a compliment," Relli said.

"Right."

"I got all the respect in the world for your mother. I just want you to know that."

"I'm sure it's mutual," said Bobby. Relli shot him a look, trying to figure out if the kid was being snotty, but Bobby had a straight face.

There was another silence, and then Relli said, "You a sports fan? I got a box at Tiger Stadium you wanna go to a ball game sometime."

"Sure," said Bobby. "That'd be good."

"I played a little ball when I was a kid," said Relli. "The Tigers wanted to give me a contract, send me to Toledo. But I went to work for your grandfather instead. I mean, why go down to Triple A when you can start out in the majors. Am I right?"

"Absolutely," said Bobby.

"I was a lefty," said Relli, making a batting gesture with his hands. "What about you?"

"Only in politics," said Bobby. It slipped out, and he regretted it immediately. The way to play this game was to agree with everything and say nothing; provocative remarks only prolonged the agony.

"Yeah, I noticed you got long hair," said Relli. "Not that it means that much these days. Hell, I seen a Bonanno button with a ponytail last time I was in Vegas, and he ain't no homo, I guarantee you that. So you, what, voted for McGovern?"

"I was too young to vote."

"I'm a Nixon guy all the way. That Watergate thing, that was a frame-up. Same as they done to Agnew."

Bobby shrugged. "I didn't follow it."

"Yeah, what for? When I was your age all I cared about was money and pussy." Relli caught himself and glanced with alarm in the direction of the kitchen. "I'm talkin' years ago," he said.

Bobby nodded and watched Relli run a blunt finger around his shirt collar. Although the house was air-conditioned, he looked hot and uncomfortable. "Your mom tells me you just finished school."

"Right."

"That's good. You gotta get your education when you're young. Then you can learn the rest on the streets, so to speak.

Like, you can study music in school, but you gotta go into the clubs to get your chops. Am I right?"

Bobby nodded. He was glad this moron was with his mother. She deserved him.

"Nixon was like that. He got there the hard way. But you know the thing I like most about him? He stood up. He never ratted anybody out. In my book, that's the worst thing you can do." There was a long pause; Bobby was aware that Relli was scrutinizing him. "You feel the same way, Bob?"

"I haven't thought much about it."

"Yeah, well you should. Squealing is the lowest thing a guy can do, especially when it's on his friends."

Bobby nodded.

"I mean, let's be realistic here. Let's be fair. You got a guy, he's maybe a made man or he's connected, the point is, he's doing business. And then he gets his balls in a ringer and the first thing you know he's fucking Tony Bennett. Perry Como. See what I'm saying? A guy who sings on his friends . . . " Relli pounded his right fist into the palm of his left hand. "You mind if I take another drink?"

"Help yourself," said Bobby.

Relli went to the liquor cabinet and poured himself a Chivas refill. Then he settled back on the couch and said, "You'd be shocked at who turns rat. When you get to be my age, that's one of the things that's gonna disillusion you about your fellow human beings. Joe Valachi, for example. Or Jimmy Hoffa."

Relli's intense stare was disconcerting. Bobby cleared his throat and waited.

"I see you're surprised I mentioned Hoffa," said Relli. "I guess you haven't heard."

Bobby shook his head.

"Jimmy's gone nuts. He's pissed off about not getting his old job back, so he's threatening to talk to the feds. He does that, a lot of good people get hurt." Relli lowered his voice for emphasis and said, "Including your own family. Over the years the Tuccis have done a lot of business with the Teamsters. What Hoffa knows could put the don in trouble. I'd hate to see him spend his last days on earth gettin' dicked around by the fuckin' FBI."

"Yeah, that would be too bad," said Bobby.

"Fuckin' right," said Relli. He still couldn't decide if this Bobby was a flake, like his mother said, or just a cold-blooded little bastard. Either way, he had made a promise to Annette. "It's not just the don, either. Hoffa talks, your mom's gonna get dragged in. They always go after the women, those federal creeps. They know that's where the weak link is."

Bobby couldn't resist. "My mother ought to come as quite a shock to them, then," he said. When Relli scowled, he added, "I mean, I don't think you could describe her as weak, do you?"

"She's a stand-up lady," said Relli. "But she's got a mother's heart. She's worried about you."

"Me?"

"Sure, you. Once the feds get going, you think they're gonna let the don's only grandson off the hook?"

Bobby laughed. "I've never met Jimmy Hoffa in my life."

"There's such a thing as a frame-up," said Relli darkly. "They could use you to get the don to talk, or your mom. It happens all the time."

Bobby felt a flash of fear. Then he remembered what his grandfather had told him: Believe no one. "I guess I'll just have to take my chances," he said.

Relli leaned forward and said, "It ain't gonna come to that. Hoffa ain't gonna talk to nobody."

"I thought you just said he was."

"I said he intends to. The powers that be got other plans."

Bobby shifted uncomfortably. "Why are you telling me this?"

This was Relli's moment. He had danced the kid around enough; it was time to make his pitch. "You know, me and your dad was very close," he said. "I was right there with him when he keeled over at the hockey game. You know what his last words to me were? He said, 'Keep an eye on my son.'" Relli stole a peek at the kid's face. His expression was hard to read, but Relli could tell he was moved. "That's what he said, swear to God. So now, here comes this no-good fuck Hoffa, out to destroy your grampa and your mom and you, and I gotta ask myself, what would Roberto want me to do?" He paused, waiting for Bobby's response.

Bobby was tempted to say, "You don't get an answer to a rhetorical question, you dumbass." Instead he merely said, "What?"

"I think you already know the answer to that, Bob," said Relli. "You're a Tucci, it's in your blood. Your dad would want me to help you save your mom and your grampa. He'd say, 'Al, when you do what you gotta do, take my boy with you. Give him the chance to do the right thing for his family.' "

Bobby gulped. "Let me get this straight. You're going to kill Jimmy Hoffa, and you want me to help?"

Relli winced at the boy's callow stupidity. "I don't need your help, Bob, that's not the point. You know how many guys would kill for the chance to get in on this? We're not talking about doin' the job on some eggplant dope man. This is a fuckin' historical hit, like Kennedy or Bugsy Siegel. The guys who do this are gonna be made for life." He spread his hands, palms up, and said, "That's what Roberto woulda wanted for you."

"How about my mother?" asked Bobby. "Is this what she wants, too?"

"Is *what* what she wants?" asked Annette. She had come out of the kitchen wearing a burnt-orange leisure suit and matching lipstick, mules with five-inch stilleto heels, and a Cutty Sark–induced grin.

"I was just telling Bobby about the Hoffa deal," said Relli.

"It sounds kind of cool," Bobby said, automatically slipping into his agreeable-fool persona. "I mean, just being able to say I took part in something like that."

Relli squirmed himself into a corkscrew. "What are you, nuts? You do this, you can't say shit to anybody. Ever."

"Then how will people know?" asked Bobby. "I mean, you said whoever does it will be made for life. How will he be made for life if nobody knows it was him?"

"Don't worry, the right people are gonna know without being told," said Relli.

"I don't see how that could be," Bobby said. "Anybody could take the credit."

"Christ, look at this kid," said Relli. "He's got a question for everything."

Annette fixed her son with a maternal glare and said, "Al has all my confidence. He's going out of his way for you, here. The least you can do is give him the respect."

"Sorry," Bobby said contritely. "Is it okay if I think it over?"

"Think during dinner," said Annette, motioning them to the dining room. "I got something special for you tonight."

Relli brightened instantly; all the talk had made him hungry. "Your mom's a sensational cook," he told Bobby. "She's got me eating things I never even knew about. You ever heard of greathead?"

A joke sprang to mind, but Bobby stifled it and shook his head.

"It's a fish. Delicious."

"Tonight we're having *kodai no shioyaki*," said Annette. "That means 'salt-broiled porgy' in Japanese."

"Like *Porgy and Bess*," said Relli. Now that he was finished talking to Bobby he was in a jolly mood. He'd made good on his promise to Annette; what the kid decided didn't really make much difference to him.

"It looks like it's swimming," said Bobby.

"That's 'cause the skewers force it into a curve," said Annette. "Johnny Baldini showed me how to do it."

"Baldini's a fruit fly," said Relli, digging into his fish. "I don't know why you bother with him."

"He's a great goddamn chef, that's why. We're thinking about opening a Japanese restaurant. Right now we're experimenting, putting a menu together."

"Hey, Bobby, looks like we're just a couple of guinea pigs," said Relli. He took a slug of Sapporo straight from the bottle and laughed. "Baby, this Jap fish is fantastic. You can experiment on me anytime."

"Don't worry," said Annette, "I got a few more recipes I plan to try out on you. You big Guinea pig."

Chapter Fifteen

AFTER DINNER BOBBY stopped at a Sunoco station and called Tillie. "How was it?" she asked.

"Just a typical evening with Annette Tucci, all-American mom," said Bobby.

"Seriously."

"I'll tell you about it when I get there. Meantime, I need Mendy's number. It's in the book next to the phone in the kitchen."

"He's not home."

"How do you know?"

"He called just after you left to find out what my mother's favorite flower is. He wanted to buy her a corsage."

"A corsage? You're shitting me."

"They went dancing. I wouldn't wait up for him tonight."

"In that case I think I'll stay down here, get over to the deli first thing in the morning."

"Sure, stay out all night," said Tillie. She lowered the receiver and yelled, "Hey, Ramón, fix me another brandy Alexander. Don't worry, Bobby's not coming back."

"Very funny. Listen, I should be up there by ten, ten-thirty tomorrow morning. Wait for me at home, okay?"

"You all right? You sound freaked out."

"I am, a little. Actually, more than a little. I'll tell you tomorrow."

"You sure? I could drive down."

"Let me talk to Mendy first," said Bobby. "And tell Ramón he better be careful, I know a guy who'll give him a pair of cement cha-cha boots for the price of a Japanese fish dinner."

Bobby spent the night at the Holiday Inn off Michigan Avenue. He arose at six, took a quick shower, smoked a joint to calm his nerves, and drove the few blocks to the Bull Pen. When he got there he saw a patrol car out front and a small curious crowd peering into the deli. He felt a flash of fear, but when he pushed his way in Mendy was sitting calmly at the counter, sipping coffee and chatting with a cop. A nun and a dozen or so well-behaved kindergarten kids sat nearby, eating cereal from plastic bowls.

In the rear of the deli another policeman was talking to a sullen young guy around Bobby's age. He was tall, six-two at least, and muscular. His forearms were tattooed, and there was blood on his white T-shirt.

"Hey, Bobby," said Mendy brightly. "How about some breakfast? I got flapjacks."

"No, thanks. What's happening?"

"It already happened," said the first cop, a beefy, red-faced young guy with a beginner's mustache. "Mendy cold-cocked Roger over there."

"Aw, he's just a junkie from the neighborhood. How about a cup of coffee at least?"

Bobby shook his head. "What'd he do?"

"He came in and started cursing," said Mendy. "I asked him to leave, but . . ." He shrugged his shoulders.

"So you kicked his ass and called the cops," said Bobby.

Mendy blinked and ducked his head. "Hey, I'd never do that."

"Would you believe Roger called himself?" said the cop with glee. He had a great station house story, and he was happy to rehearse it. "He reports an assault and battery. When we get here he's out in the parking lot with blood all over his face. He starts telling us what happened, and my partner says, 'Man, if I was you I'd be too embarrassed to admit I got my ass kicked by a guy that old.'"

"I caught him with a sneak punch," said Mendy. "It's an old fighter's trick."

"You were a professional fighter?" asked Bobby. "I never knew that."

"Sure. Everybody was a fighter back then," Mendy said. "Mostly I just fought smokers against my cousin. His name's Mendy Pearlstein, too."

"That must have confused 'em," said the cop.

"Nah, one of us was always Kid Kennedy. We switched off. It didn't make no difference, the fights was all fixed anyhow."

"Well, you still got a hell of a punch," said the cop. "Roger lost three teeth, and he's gonna need stitches."

"You're not going to press charges, are you?" asked Bobby.

The cop gave Bobby an incredulous look and said, "Against Mendy?"

When the cops were gone, Bobby said, "There's something we need to talk about."

"I hope this ain't about Tillie's mom," Mendy said with a guilty grin.

"It's about *my* mom. I had dinner with her and a guy named Alberto Relli last night. You know him?"

"Sure."

"He's going to kill Jimmy Hoffa, and he invited me to come along for the ride. According to him, it's a real career opportunity."

Mendy sat down slowly on one of the plastic-covered counter stools. "Jeez, you knocked the wind outta me," he said.

"He says Hoffa's going to testify against—well, I don't know exactly against who, but the contract's supposed to be from the National Commission, whatever that is."

"I know Jimmy since he was a kid bagging groceries at Kroger's out in Pontiac," said Mendy. "No way he'd talk, not in a million years."

"I'm just repeating what I was told. Maybe it's bogus. He's hot to impress my mother."

"I better call your grampa," Mendy said. He poured Bobby a Coke from the fountain, went to the kitchen, dialed

Vittorio's number, and spoke briefly. Then he came back frowning.

"What's the matter?" asked Bobby.

"Catello says he's not feeling strong enough to talk right now."

"Catello? What happened to Carlo Seluchi? He's the one who usually answers the phone."

Mendy shrugged. "He said Seluchi's out in Vegas."

"You don't believe him?"

"Seluchi's been your grampa's driver for twenty years. I don't see him going on vacation at a time like this."

"How about talking to Catello, then?" asked Bobby. "He's consigliere."

"Listen, I know two things for sure. One, your grampa wouldn't want you mixed up in a hit on Jimmy Hoffa. And two, Catello's a snake."

"Okay, but right now Relli's the problem. Maybe Catello could help."

"Everybody's the problem," said Mendy. "What we gotta do is keep our eyes open and play dumb until we figure out what's what."

"Maybe we should get out of town until things blow over," said Bobby. "Me and Tillie. Just split."

Mendy shrugged.

"Why not?"

"Out of town there's the whole world to get in trouble in. This is home court."

"It's Relli's home court, too."

"Yeah, but I been playin' on it for so long, we might have a little advantage."

Bobby put down his Coke and said, "If this wasn't so serious it would be funny. My whole life I've been trying to avoid the Family, and now—one dinner and I'm in the middle of a hit on Jimmy Hoffa."

Mendy blinked, coughed, and said, "Bobby, that guy Roger? When I smacked him I was wearing these." He held up a pair of brass knuckles.

"No wonder you knocked his teeth out."

"In this kind of fighting there's no rules. Especially with bosses like Relli and Catello. You use what you got."

"Great," said Bobby. "What do we have?"

Mendy said, "We got each other."

"You think that's going to be enough?"

Mendy shrugged. "Jeez. I dunno. I've never been up against guys like them before."

Chapter Sixteen

IT TOOK THE combined efforts of John Bertoia, Hedda Hopper, and the Mouse for Luigi Catello to put the pieces together and figure out what was happening right under his nose.

First came Bertoia's information: Relli was spending a lot of time at the home of Annette Tucci. Bertoia, Alberto Relli's cousin, was Catello's informer in the Relli regime. The father of six, he intended to have a job no matter who won in the Tucci Family's war of succession.

Next, Hedda Hopper came to town. Hedda's real name was Chuckie Fina, and he occupied a unique place in the landscape of American crime as the mafia's unofficial but universally recognized gossip columnist.

Fina was a handsome, personable young man, the scion of

a respected Staten Island family, whose parents were killed in a traffic accident on the Triboro Bridge when he was eleven. For the next ten years he bounced around among adoring aunts in Los Angeles, Brooklyn, St. Louis, and Miami. All Chuckie's relatives were connected, and soon the peripatetic boy with the long eyelashes, sweet smile, and tragic story became well known in mafia circles across the country.

It was the time of the McClellan hearings; people were nervous about writing letters or talking on the telephone. They began asking Chuckie to pass along bits of information—the engagement of an underboss's daughter, an aging don's successful hernia operation, a consigliere's plan to build a new house in the suburbs—to friends and relations in the cities he visited. The information was innocuous, but no one wanted to unwittingly give the government even the slightest bit of help.

Soon Chuckie, with his keen eye for personal detail, became a much awaited messenger. Not only did he announce engagements, but he gave amusing accounts of the courtship, embellished medical news with tidbits of bedside gossip, and brought word of new styles of dress, architecture, and home decor in the various Families.

"This kid hops off a plane, tells me things about my own brother I never even knew, and then he hops back on the plane and disappears," Don Alphonse Almonte of Portland once remarked, and it gave birth to Chuckie's nickname: Hedda Hopper.

As he grew into manhood, gossipmongering became

Chuckie's full-time occupation. Luigi Catello was one of the first who saw his intelligence value. Catello cultivated him with small confidences and unfailing courtesy and, in return, he often got information more valuable than wedding announcements or fashion tips. This is how he learned that something big was about to happen in Detroit around the end of July. Hedda Hopper didn't know what it would be, but he had heard that the National Commission was involved.

Catello's next step was to get Mouse Campanella to bug Annette Tucci's house.

Mouse was a reluctant electronics wizard. As a boy his 152 IQ had been a source of wonder to his parents, simple people who ran a Tucci Family numbers operation in Pontiac; but for Mouse himself, his brains had been a curse. He did not have a scholarly temperament, and he resented the expectations and demands of his teachers. He also despised the goody-goodies in his advanced classes. From an early age Mouse Campanella was determined to find antisocial uses for his intellectual gifts.

Unlike most guys with his nickname, Mouse didn't look like one. He was of average height, with a powerful upper body, a dark complexion, and jet-black hair worn in a crew cut. He got the name in high school for performing "mousectomies"—recreational brain surgery on stolen laboratory mice.

After graduation, Mouse enlisted in the navy, where his IQ got him assigned to radio school and then to a spy ship off the coast of Vietnam. His talent for snooping won him a promotion; his involvement in drug smuggling got him two years in a military prison and a dishonorable discharge.

Mouse returned to Pontiac, where he used his parents' contacts to gain an appointment with Luigi Catello. The consigliere was immediately impressed by the young veteran's technical expertise and larcenous character and offered him a job. In just three years he worked his way up from entry level to running the communications facilities in the basement of the Tucci mansion. Most young men would have been satisfied, but Mouse was ambitious. He knew that he could rise only so high in the Family as a technician; the senior posts would always be reserved for made men, well-rounded mobsters with street credentials. This he knew from Catello himself.

Despite the difference in their ages and status, Mouse and Catello became close. They shared a taste for fast food and the slow women who serve it. And they were both avid hunters. Every autumn they spent a long weekend at the Tucci Family's private preserve in northern Michigan, where they mowed down deer from a jeep equipped with mounted machine guns. As their friendship deepened, Catello spoke to his protégé with rare frankness about Tucci politics. So when Mouse played the tape of Relli and Bobby Tucci discussing a hit on Jimmy Hoffa, he was unsurprised by Catello's reaction: "That rotten prick Relli. We had a deal."

"We going to BOB?" asked Mouse. BOB stood for Brains Over Brawn. It was Catello's contingency plan for eliminating Alberto Relli and installing himself as the new don.

Catello stroked his double chin. "This Hoffa thing is a new wrinkle," he said. "If the Commission gave the contract to the don, and the don gave it to Relli, that's bad."

"How about tipping off Hoffa? Let him take care of the Relli problem."

Catello shook his head. "I can't go up against the Commission. They find out I dropped a dime, I'm a dead man. We gotta take Relli out in a way that don't seem like a hit. Then I step in, handle the Hoffa contract myself, and everything's tied up in a neat package."

"What about Bobby? If he goes along with Relli, he's gonna have a claim."

"I'm more worried about his old lady," said Catello. "Bobby's just a kid. If Relli's talking to him, Annette's behind it. That means we gotta neutralize her."

The Mouse laughed. "There's a lot of guys around who would volunteer to whack her out. I wouldn't mind myself."

"You're not thinking," Catello said. "Annette gets whacked, we got her old man to deal with. No, this thing has to go by the numbers, one step at a time. Step number one, ask Joey Florio to come see me."

Dr. Joey Florio was in the midst of a postcoital afternoon nap in the upstairs infirmary when Mouse called. "I'll stop by tomorrow morning," he said grumpily.

"Don't worry, I'll tell Eileen I'm working late and we can go to Joe Muir's for dinner," said Mouse. "Fucking you makes me want to eat a juicy lobster."

"What?"

Mouse repeated himself in an expressionless voice and waited for Florio to recognize his own words; they were the last thing he said to Nurse Felice before dozing off.

"Fucking spook," Florio said. "Shit. Okay, I'll be down in fifteen minutes."

"Make it ten," said Mouse, hanging up.

Florio arrived red-faced with anger. "Bugging my clinic isn't going to do you a fucking bit of good," he told Catello. "You think I care if Eileen knows about me and Felice? Give me the phone, I'll call her myself and tell her."

"Come on, Joey, you know I'd never blackmail you," said Catello. "Tell me, how's the don doing?"

"You got me out of bed for that?"

"It's important to me, Joey."

"He's doing all right," said Florio, unable to stifle his professional pride. "He's responding to the protocol."

"He could live to a hundred," said Catello. "Right?"

"Six months at the outside," said Florio. "But these are six months he wouldn't have if he wasn't getting the right treatment."

"You told Annette," said Catello.

"Like hell I did. I don't talk to Annette."

"You want me to play you the conversation?"

"She's got a right to know," said Florio defensively. "She's his daughter-in-law."

"Joey, you're a bright man and I'm not going to insult your intelligence," said Catello. "Since you're taking from Annette, obviously the money you get from me isn't big enough to buy your loyalty. So we're going to change the nature of our relationship. Let me start with a simple question: How's the don doing?"

"I just told you, he's doing okay," said Florio cautiously. He was one of the few members of the Tucci Family who knew how the fat consigliere had risen to power.

"I think he'd be better off in a coma," said Catello.

"What?"

"Maybe 'coma' ain't the right word," Catello conceded. "Laymen talk medicine, it sometimes comes out wrong. What I want is for you to make him unconscious and keep him unconscious until I tell you to pull the plug. After the funeral you receive a million-dollar severance package and get lost. That's clearer, right?"

"I'm a doctor, not some fucking greaseball hit man," said Florio. He was shaking; Catello wasn't sure if it was from anger or fear.

"If that's what you tell yourself, that's fine," Catello said mildly. "Mouse!"

Mouse Campanella came into Catello's office. He was carrying a Smith & Wesson .38 with a silencer. Florio began shaking harder. Now Catello was sure it was fear.

"The Mouse has been after me to let him make his bones," Catello said in a matter-of-fact way. "So either you do what I tell you or he's going to shoot you and toss your body in a lime pit. Right, Mouse?"

Mouse nodded; he was ready.

Florio took a deep breath, trying to collect himself. If he disappeared, there would be questions, but he knew Catello would have answers. "What about Annette? What do I tell her?"

Catello shrugged. "Tell her the truth, that the don's out. She wants to see him, that's okay."

"What if she brings in another doctor?"

"Use something another doc won't pick up on," said Catello. "You got medicine like that?"

Reluctantly, Florio nodded.

"Good. And don't worry, I'll see to it there's no autopsy."

"How about Seluchi? What if he wants to take the don to a hospital?"

Catello's round face broke into a smile. "Seluchi is on his way to that lime pit I just mentioned. You hurry, you can catch up to him. Or you can walk away a millionaire. You've got five seconds to choose."

Florio saw Mouse looking at his watch with a hungry expression. "Okay, okay," he said.

"That's great, Joey," said Catello. "You're too good a man to die over something like this. Mouse, go upstairs, kick the nurse out, and get things ready."

Mouse flashed the doctor a resentful look and left with his head down.

"Did you know that his IQ is one fifty-two?" said Catello. "He could get into Mensa if he wanted to. You happen to know your IQ?"

Florio shook his head.

"I don't know mine, either. Hey, look, Mouse is going to film you in the clinic. Just tell the camera what you're doing. Give details, the type of medicine and all. Then he'll film the don once he's unconscious. That plus the tape of this conversation will be enough to keep you honest. I don't mean to insult you, but you did try to fuck me before with Annette. This time we both know how things stand. Okay?"

"Do I have a choice?"

"I'm afraid of that attitude," said Catello. "I want you to be happy, not angry. Because if you're not happy you'll be dangerous. And if I think you're dangerous, you're going to wind up in a place that makes the lime pit seem like fuckin' Bermuda. So, let me ask you one more time. Are we okay?"

"We're okay," said Florio.

"You're happy?"

"I'm happy."

"Good," said Catello cheerfully. "Now I only got one problem left."

Florio said, "What's that?"

"I gotta find the Mouse somebody else to kill."

Chapter
Seventeen

ANNETTE LEFT THE don's mansion with Alberto Relli. They had seen with their own eyes that the old man was unconscious, heard Dr. Florio say the odds were he wouldn't be back. "You've got to handle the Hoffa contract before he kicks," said Annette. "Otherwise the whole succession thing gets thrown into an uproar."

"I already thought of that," said Relli. "I got a meet with Little Jimmy all set up."

"Don't forget Bobby."

"Hey, I promised," Relli said. "Tomorrow me and Bertoia are gonna walk through the hit. Tell Bobby to meet me at noon at the Sav-on Drugs at Maple and Telegraph. He can tag along."

"He'll be there," said Annette. She pressed her lips to Relli's ear and whispered, "Don Alberto."

Relli put his hand on Annette's behind, but she moved away. "Somebody will see us," she said. "Come by my place after you do Hoffa, and we'll really have a party. Johnny Baldini's got this new fish that costs four hundred dollars a pound. I'll have him cook it up for us while we're making love, and we can eat it for dessert."

"What the hell do we need Baldini for?"

"He's the don's chef, right? So he's gonna belong to you. You might as well get used to him. Don't worry, he won't bother us."

"Whatever you say, babe," said Relli. He was too happy to argue. He had everything a man could look forward to. In just a few days he would pull off the hit of the century, become head of the Tucci Family, and then celebrate his good fortune with a four-hundred-buck fish and a million-dollar blow job.

WHEN MENDY OPENED the door to his apartment Bobby said, "Are you all alone?"

"Sure. Come on in."

"With you I never know who I'll find," said Bobby. "A niece, a showgirl, a nun, Tillie's mother—"

"Hey, I never been with a nun in my life," said Mendy.

Bobby's expression grew serious. "I'm supposed to meet Relli tomorrow in a strip mall in West Bloomfield. There's some restaurant out there where Relli's planning to meet Hoffa."

"The hit's tomorrow?"

Bobby shook his head. "Tomorrow's just the dress rehearsal. Jesus, I can't believe I'm actually sitting here talking about this. It's so fucking weird."

"What did you tell your mom? About going with Relli?"

"I told her sure, I'd meet him."

"Good. Go along for the ride, see what's what. Then we can figure out our next move. I hope."

"Me, too," said Bobby. He took a deep breath and said, "You know something? I'm scared, I admit it."

"Jeez," said Mendy.

"But I guess it's only natural. I mean, anybody would be scared in this situation. Right?"

Mendy shrugged. "I bet Relli ain't scared," he said.

M OUSE WAS IN the basement of the mansion working the *New York Times* crossword when Catello came in and said, "I just heard from Bertoia. Tomorrow's your big day."

"Kind of short notice," said Mouse.

"Forget it, then, somebody else can do it. Some other ambitious young comer." When Mouse flushed with anger, Catello said, "Don't get your bowels in an uproar, I'm just kidding."

"I don't see the humor," said Mouse.

"Relax, I got everything all worked out. Tomorrow after the walk-through, Relli and Bertoia are gonna drop Bobby off and head out to Pine Lake. Dean Martin's there, and Relli's invited for drinks before the show. On the way they're gonna stop at the Family warehouse in Pontiac, so that Relli can pick up a new sound system for his Cadillac. There won't be anybody there but you. They arrive, Bertoia shoots Relli in the head, stuffs him in the trunk, drives him up to the farm in Washtenaw County, and buries him in the cornfield. Simple as it gets."

"Where do I come in?"

"On the way out to the farm get Bertoia to brief you on the details of the Hoffa job—where, when, what. When you get to the farm, he's gonna dig a grave. Give him a hand, then shoot him in the back of the head and dump him along with Relli. Afterwards dispose of Relli's car. I'll leave that one up to you." Catello paused; he was beaming at Mouse with fond condescension. "A guy with your IQ, you gotta do at least a little independent thinking to make your bones."

Mouse stared at Catello in what the consigliere mistook for awe. Then he said, "Bertoia's one of us. He's on our side."

"Bertoia's a loose end," Catello said. "Not to mention a traitor. He sold out Relli and that's his own cousin; imagine what he'd do to me."

"Yeah, but—"

Catello stiffened and said, "Hey, you fuckin' mouse, I'm giving you a chance. You ain't up to it, you can rot down here in this basement."

"I'm sorry, Luigi," said Mouse. "I wasn't thinking." That was a lie. Mouse was thinking. He was thinking that when Relli and Bertoia were dead, he would be nothing but a loose end himself.

C h a p t e r
E i g h t e e n

BOBBY OPENED HIS eyes and Tillie said, "You were mumbling in your sleep."

"What'd I say?"

"Something about your mother. I hope you're not developing an Oedipus complex."

Bobby snorted and looked at his watch. "Speaking of mothers, what time are you meeting yours?"

"One-thirty."

"I can drop you off."

"I'll take the van and meet you later. She's going downtown afterward."

"Mendy?"

Tillie frowned. "I'm not so sure I like what's going on," she said. "At first it was a grunt, but it's getting a little sick. I mean, he's old enough to be her father."

"So?"

"I dreamed about them in bed together," said Tillie with a small shudder.

"You're the one who's getting oedipal," said Bobby. He slid out of bed, put Otis Redding on the stereo, and went into the bathroom to shower.

Tillie followed him in. "I wish you'd tell me what the hell's going on," she said.

"It's better if I don't," said Bobby. "Mendy thinks so, too."

"Next time you're in the mood for sex, get it from Mendy," said Tillie, and went back to bed.

Bobby made the drive from Ann Arbor to West Bloomfield in forty-five minutes. He went into Sav-on Drugs and bought the new *Rolling Stone.* There was no sign of Relli, so he sat in the Porsche reading about Eric Clapton and listening to a Falcons tape. He was so absorbed in Clapton's problems that the sound of a heavy metal ring clinking against his window made him jump. He looked up and saw the dark, uneven features of Alberto Relli grinning through the glass.

"Relax, kid," said Relli. "Hey, what kind of stereo you got?"

"Sony," said Bobby.

"Is it any good? I can't tell with that jig music you got playing."

Bobby nodded. "But it's not just the stereo, it's the speakers. You have to get the whole system right."

"That's somethin' to remember," Relli said. "You ready to roll?"

"Are we taking my car?"

Relli laughed. "I'd have to hack Hoffa up like a fuckin' Caesar salad just to get him in the backseat."

Relli led Bobby to his Cadillac, where Bertoia was waiting behind the wheel. Bobby knew him by sight and nodded. Relli pointed to a building at the far end of the parking lot. The sign read: MACHUS RED FOX. "You know this place?" he asked.

"I've passed it," said Bobby. "I've never eaten there, though."

"It don't cater to the college crowd," said Bertoia.

"Okay, let's run through this," said Relli. "Bertoia, you be Hoffa."

"Whaddya mean, be Hoffa?"

"Be Hoffa," Relli repeated in an exasperated tone. "You pull in, I'm waiting in the parking lot. I wave and come over. You open the window. Go ahead, open it."

Bertoia opened his window. Relli got out of the car, came around to the driver's side and leaned in. "Hey, Jimmy, right on time."

Bertoia looked blank. "Say something, dummy," Relli snapped.

"Like what?"

"Say, 'How's the wife and kids?' Hoffa's always askin' about the wife and kids."

"Hey, how's the wife and kids?" Bertoia said. He had a disgusted expression on his face.

"Good, Jimmy, how's yours?"

"They're all fuckin' dead," said Bertoia. "They got hit by fuckin' lightning."

"Hey, that's good to hear, blah blah blah. Now I say, 'Jimmy, there's this piece of farmland out Inkster Road that's about to get rezoned for a giant shopping mall.' Hoffa's a sucker for real estate. Now you ask me, 'Who else is in?' "

"Who else is in?"

"Just you, me, and Bobby."

"Who the fuck is Bobby? Right?"

Relli nodded. "Bobby Tucci, the don's grandson. He's a college boy, just getting his feet wet, but he's good people." Relli glanced at Bobby to make sure he was enjoying the show; he could imagine the kid describing it to Annette later on. "Now I point to my car and say, 'He's sitting right over there with Bertoia. Ride out with us, we can talk on the way.' "

"What about his driver?" asked Bertoia.

"Hoffa drives himself, and he don't have a bodyguard. It's a tough-guy image thing with him."

"Yeah, but it ain't just P.R.," said Bertoia. "You know how many push-ups the guy does a day? I was readin' in the *Free Press*."

"Hey, I don't know how many times he takes a dump, either," said Relli impatiently. "Listen to me. Hoffa gets in the back, I get in back with him, we're heading out into the country. We pull off at a certain spot, we get out, and I pop Hoffa in the fuckin' head. Then we stick him in a plastic bag and put him in the trunk. Bertoia, you drop me and Bobby off at the Southfield Athletic Club. We spend the afternoon there with a million witnesses while you dump the body at the farm."

Bobby said, "If somebody sees you talking in the parking lot, and they determine the time of death, won't the police put two and two together?"

"Hey, look at you, Perry Mason." Relli ruffled Bobby's hair and said, "They can't do that without the body. Come on, let's take a run. Bertoia, drive nice and easy, just the regular speed. I wanna time the trip."

The spot, off Inkster Road, was twenty minutes out and twenty-two back. When they returned to the parking lot Relli said, "Bob, I'm gonna ask you to do me a personal favor. Come with me to Pontiac, help me pick out a good stereo for my car."

"Sure," said Bobby. A ride out to Pontiac would give him the opportunity he had been looking for.

"Good. How about you let me drive the Porsche and Bertoia can follow us?"

"Why not?"

Bertoia said, "Hey, Al, I gotta make a phone call."

"Bullshit," said Relli. "You can call your fuckin' bookie from the warehouse. Let's go." He climbed into the sports car, turned the engine over, and said, "Smooth." Then he reached into his jacket pocket and handed Bobby a cassette.

"What's this?"

"*Dino's Greatest Hits*," said Relli, wheeling the Porsche onto Maple Road. "Something a white man can hum along to."

Bobby said, "I want to thank you for letting me in on all this. It's really exciting."

"Hey, a promise is a promise." Relli checked the rearview to make sure Bertoia was following. "What'd you think of my plan?"

"I'm no expert, but it seems very realistic."

"Bob, it don't get more realistic than this," Relli said.

"That's so cool. I can't believe I'm going to get to see a real mafia hit. I'll bet Mario Puzo never did."

"Puzo, the guy wrote *The Godfather*?"

"Right."

"Why'dya mention him?"

"Just the name of another writer that came to mind."

"Another writer? Who's the *other* writer?" Relli looked at Bobby sideways and said, "Don't tell me it's you."

"I haven't actually published anything yet," Bobby said modestly. "What I really want to do is screenplays."

Relli made a sound in his throat like an electric drill boring into a cantaloupe. "You ain't thinkin' of writing about this," he said. It was not a question.

"Course not," said Bobby. "I mean, I might use some basic details, but I'd change everything around so that nobody would get into trouble. Like, I'd set it in, um, let's say Buffalo or Pittsburgh. The victim could be in the Steelworkers Union, not the Teamsters. Maybe instead of the farm he gets dumped at sea. Trust me, nobody will ever guess—"

Relli glanced at the long-haired rich kid prattling on in the passenger seat and silently cursed himself for agreeing to take him along. Bobby caught the look on Relli's face and smiled inwardly. So much for his career as a junior hit man. Relli would never let him within a million miles of the Hoffa assassination now.

AS THEY PASSED the Miracle Mile shopping center on the outskirts of Pontiac, Alberto Relli was already formulating a new plan. Bobby Tucci was going to die in the Hoffa assassination. There was no other way to play it, even if he wanted to—the kid already knew way too much. Annette would probably be pissed and upset for a while, but she'd understand; these things happened.

Relli checked the rearview once again and saw Bertoia two cars behind. He felt a twinge of regret that he'd have to whack Bertoia, too, but he couldn't kill the don's grandson and leave a witness. He turned down the music and said, "You ever catch any of Dino's movies?"

Bobby shook his head.

"You should, he's a hell of an actor. Okay, here's the warehouse." He pointed to a large redbrick building next to some railroad tracks. Relli turned into the driveway, waited for Bertoia to pass him, and followed him around back. Bertoia opened the loading dock door with a remote and drove into the dark building. Relli followed.

Bertoia's hands were sweating as he switched off the engine. Catello hadn't said anything about Bobby Tucci coming along. He decided that he would shoot Relli as planned and then he and the Mouse could tie up Bobby and bring him out to the farm. From there they would get in touch with Catello and find out what to do with the kid. He parked the Cadillac and took his Magnum .357 from under the seat. The next step would be simple; just walk directly up to Relli and shoot him in the face. He decided he'd wait until Relli left the car. Bertoia didn't want to accidentally hit Bobby or damage the Porsche.

Mouse Campanella hid in the shadows in the rear of the warehouse and watched the scene unfold. He recognized Bobby Tucci's Porsche and wondered what the hell *he* was doing here. Typical, Mouse decided: a fuckup. He was constantly amazed at the sheer incompetence of the Tucci Family's operatives.

Mouse felt a flush of exasperation. Catello should have let him hit Relli instead of relegating him to the role of grave digger and second gun, simply because he had no hands-on experience. Bertoia's fuckup showed how much so-called experience was worth. It was something to remember when he became consigliere. For now, though, there was nothing to do but hunker down and observe.

Relli honked loudly, but there was no response. "Where the fuck is everybody?" he muttered. "They were supposed to be here to show me fuckin' stereos."

Bobby stifled a snort. One of the many things he disliked about wiseguys was their chronic cheapness. Relli was probably a multimillionaire, but he was willing to drive all the way out to Pontiac to save a couple hundred bucks on a hot car stereo. His old man had been the same way; he never paid for an appliance in his life.

Relli opened the door and swung his legs out of the Porsche. Suddenly he swiveled and looked hard at Bobby, who said, "What the matter?"

"It's a trap," said Relli softly. "Bertoia's a fuckin' traitor." He pulled a pistol from his shoulder holster as Bertoia walked quickly toward them with his arm outstretched. There was a flash of light followed by a thunderous reverberation and the sound of a man screaming. The man, Bobby realized after a moment, was him. He opened his eyes and saw that Relli was gone. He sat, frozen with fear, the voice of Dean Martin crooning in the background. The keys were still in the ignition.

Suddenly there were more explosions. Bobby jumped behind the wheel, backed out, put it in first, and burned rubber onto Telegraph Road. He was shaking so badly that he was all the way to Twelve Mile Road before he was steady enough to eject Dean Martin and toss him out the window.

Mouse watched Bobby peel away. He waited a long time in the dark, listening, but there were no sounds. The warehouse stank of cordite. He drew his pistol and walked tentatively toward the Cadillac. Alberto Relli and John Bertoia lay dead on the ground, not more than six feet from each other. Bertoia's face was blown away, but Relli's was still intact, his mouth formed in an *O* of childlike perplexity.

Mouse shook his head; Relli was supposed to be the toughest guy in the Family. He closed the warehouse and walked to his car, a '67 Mustang parked on the other side of the railroad tracks, next to a thirsty-looking elm. He was glad that disposing of the bodies—and deciding what to do with Bobby Tucci—would be Catello's problem. It left him free to concentrate his 152-megawatt IQ on the thing that mattered most: how to convince Catello to let him make his bones on Jimmy Hoffa.

Chapter Nineteen

THE FUNERAL OF Don Vittorio Tucci was the biggest event in the history of Detroit's underworld. The cathedral was flooded with flowers and packed with three thousand mourners: made members of the Tucci Family, hangers-on, assorted high rollers, middlemen, and lowlifes. Delegates from crime families throughout the country and as far away as Sicily mixed uncomfortably with a large contingent of reporters and a few highly visible agents of the FBI.

Most of the mourners, though, were the little people whom Don Vittorio had touched in his seventy-four years on earth. Some, like the Sicilian sisters who cooked for the Great Man, rent the decorum of the mass with their sobbing. Others, beneficiaries of the don's largesse who had never been allowed to forget it, sat dry-eyed, wondering who would take his place and inherit their markers. More than a few were there to silently celebrate the passing of the man who had visited some terrible injustice on them or their loved ones.

In the front pew sat Annette and Bobby Tucci, Tommy the Neck, and Luigi Catello. As consigliere, Catello had presided over the funeral arrangements, taken care of the out-of-town delegations, and seen to the details of the actual interment. There was no autopsy; everyone understood that the don had died in a coma induced by his advanced lymphoma. It was a sign of the Tuccis' confidence in Dr. Joey Florio that he was seated with the next of kin in the front pew.

Usually when Joey Florio attended a funeral he came prepared for the possibility that he would be called upon to treat some distraught, grief-stricken relative. Looking at the Tucci family, however, he was confident that today his services would not be needed. Bobby was pale and somewhat glassy-eyed—Florio could tell from the aroma of marijuana coming off the kid's black suit coat that he was stoned. Annette seemed composed to the point of indifference. Tommy the Neck stood facing the rear of the church, scanning the crowd for friends. Only Catello seemed moved by the death of the don.

As he gazed at Vittorio Tucci's coffin, Joey Florio conceded that his course of treatment might have been ethically questionable. Still, in the larger scheme of things, he had no regrets. After all, the don was going to die anyway, and soon. Getting himself thrown into a lime pit could not have helped the old man in any way. He had merely operated in accordance with his new motto: Two deaths don't make a life.

Florio had eased the old man out gently. Thirty milligrams of liquid Valium in his evening cognac had put him into an unarousable sleep. Twice-a-day pentobarbital and scopolamine-powder suppositories had kept him that way. Then, when Catello had given him the word, he had sent the don to heaven with a triple dose. Even if there had been an autopsy, it would have revealed nothing. Only a blood test could have disclosed the amount of barbiturates in Don Vittorio's system, and no one administered postmortem blood tests to seventy-four-year-old lymphoma victims.

Actually, Florio felt, he could congratulate himself on his humane treatment. Don Vittorio Tucci was a man who could have died a violent, brutal death in the streets or suffered a horrible, pain-wracked demise at the hands of his cancer. Instead, he lay in his casket with a beatific smile on his lipless, waxen countenence. The smile eased Dr. Florio's conscience; that, and the knowledge that his medical skills would soon be available to the sick and infirm of his new home, the Cayman Islands.

As the archbishop began the eulogy, Catello craned his neck, looking for Carmine "Patty Cakes" Patti. The dignitaries from the various Families sat up front, but Patti wasn't among them. A young man, not yet thirty, he was a troubleshooter for the National Commission, in Detroit to make sure that the don's death did not interfere with the Hoffa contract.

Patti was seated next to Mouse in the rear of the church. He hadn't known Don Vittorio, and he felt no sorrow at his passing. The don's death was merely a complication, and solving complications was his business. He spent most of his time gazing at the Ali MacGraw look-alike sitting across the aisle next to an old man. He concentrated his stare on her neck, trying to make her turn around. Finally she did, and smiled.

Carmine Patti was considered the most eligible bachelor in the American mafia. He was well over six feet tall, blond-haired and blue-eyed, with a straight nose and strong chin. His father was a Bonanno Family ally in Arizona. In high school and at the University of Arizona, Patti had been a foot-ball star. He got a law degree from the University of Nevada before coming east to work for the Commission. He had done such an outstanding job that he was already spoken of as a future national figure, a Frank Costello, Al Capone, or Vittorio Tucci.

Mouse noticed the exchange of smiles and nudged Patti. "That's Bobby Tucci's girl," he whispered. "Her name's Tillie."

"Thanks."

"Hey," said Mouse. He had been trying to ingratiate himself with Patti all day. At Metro Airport, when Patti asked why Alberto Relli hadn't come to pick him up, Mouse had made a knowing face and said, "Catello will explain it to you after the funeral." Patti had nodded crisply and asked no further questions. It was an executive style, terse and decisive, that Mouse found appealing, something to emulate when he became consigliere.

Catello spotted Mouse and Patti in the back of the chapel.

The consigliere had been furious at Mouse for his passivity in the warehouse, but now that he had time to think about it, he realized the situation had worked out pretty well. Better than pretty well, actually. Relli and Bertoia were up in Washtenaw County, growing with the corn, and Bobby Tucci had lost his virginity.

Catello was sensitive to the lingering damage that kidnapping Don Silvio Mossi's daughter had done to his image. Going after Vittorio Tucci's innocent college-boy grandson would have been a PR disaster. But by joining up with Relli, Bobby had become fair game.

The boy, Catello realized, held the key to his ambitions. Bobby had the two things that stood between Catello and unchallenged control of the Family—the details of the Hoffa hit, and his status as the last living Tucci. Luigi Catello fully intended to divest him of both.

Chapter
Twenty

As THE FUNERAL procession formed outside the cathedral, Carmine Patti felt Luigi Catello's pudgy hand on his elbow. "Let's ride out to the cemetery together," he said.

Patti nodded. Mouse, standing nearby, was again impressed by the tall Arizonan's cool demeanor. Compared to him, Catello was a lump of dough in sizzling olive oil. "You want me to bring the car around?" he asked.

"I'll drive," said Catello. "Wait for me at the house."

On the way to the cemetery, Catello said, "Some funeral, huh? The whole country's here."

"Everybody except Alberto Relli," said Patti evenly.

"Yeah. Poor Relli." Catello paused for dramatic effect. "He's dead."

"I thought he might be," said Patti. "How did it happen?"

"He got shot by his own cousin, Johnny Bertoia. He managed to whack Johnny back before he croaked." Catello shook his head. "Say what you want about Relli, he was a rough customer."

"What was Bertoia's beef?"

Catello shrugged his round shoulders eloquently. "Some family thing. I think maybe Al was playing around with Bertoia's wife, there was a rumor like that. Anyways, he's gone. They both are."

They drove in silence for a while, Patti looking out the window. Finally he said, "Convenient for you."

"Yeah, I can't deny it," said Catello. "Relli would have had a tough time accepting my authority over the Tuccis."

"Don Vittorio picked him, not you."

"The don never told me that."

"Maybe not, but he told the Commission."

"The Commission don't decide," said Catello. "It's a local matter."

"Unless the Commission doesn't accept the local decision," said Patti. "You know the precedents."

"You sound like a lawyer," said Catello.

"And you sound like a defendant."

"How does a defendant sound?"

"Innocent," said Patti. "Always innocent." He laughed and gave Catello a charming smile that broke the tension. "Look, Luigi, I didn't come out here to bust balls or interfere in Tucci Family business. I've only got one concern—"

"Hoffa," said Catello.

"The don told you?"

"We didn't have secrets. I got it under control. You can tell the Commission that it's gonna go right on schedule."

"I need more than that. Don Vittorio's death has made people nervous. They're going to be even more nervous when they find out Relli's dead. I can't convince them things are still all right unless I'm convinced first. You understand, right?"

Catello drove for a while in silence. Finally he said, "Relli had a meet with Hoffa coming up, which is when he was going to hit him. I got the word to Jimmy that Relli had to go to Sicily for a couple days, to protect the Family's interests now that the don's dead, but that he'll be back in time for his meet. When Hoffa shows, we'll take him out."

Patti tapped the dashboard with his manicured fingernails. "It won't work unless you know exactly what Relli set up."

"I got the details," Catello lied. "Relli filled me in before he died."

Patti gave Catello a skeptical look but said nothing. In all likelihood, the consigliere would be the next head of the Tucci Family, and it wouldn't do to call him a liar to his face. Not unless Catello had to be killed—and it was still too early to come to that conclusion. In any event, that wouldn't be Patti's call; he acted at the discretion of his client, the Commission. "Who else knows about Relli?" he asked.

"Only the Mouse."

"What about Relli's wife and kids?"

"Relli was on the revolving-door plan at home," said Catello. "He'd have to be gone for a month for his old lady to notice."

"You trust Mouse?"

"Absolutely," lied Catello once more. He had never absolutely trusted anyone in his entire life. Besides, the Mouse had punked out in the warehouse, proving he wasn't top executive material. As soon as the Hoffa business was over and he was settled in the don's mansion, the Mouse would be a candidate for permanent retirement.

"What about Bobby Tucci?" asked Patti.

"What about him?"

"I hear he's some sort of hippie."

"He's a college kid. They're all hippies."

"The old man told us he's not involved in the business."

"Correct."

"What's the story on his girlfriend?"

"She's a rich bitch from Bloomfield Hills," said Catello. "A real piece of ass. I guess you noticed."

Patti winced at the vulgarity. "Are they serious?"

"Who the fuck knows with kids? I mean, it's the fucking sexual revolution, right? That's what they say on *Phil Donahue* anyway."

"They're not engaged?"

"Not as far as I know."

They rode the rest of the way in silence. When they reached the cemetery Patti headed straight for Tillie. She looked up, saw him approaching, and grinned.

"We seem to be constantly smiling at each other," said Patti easily. "Very inappropriate for such a sad occasion, don't you think?"

"Shocking lack of decorum," Tillie agreed.

"I take it you weren't close to the deceased."

"I'm close to his grandson."

"Bobby."

"How do you know?"

"I asked. It's not a secret, is it?"

"Secret? The prince of the realm has no secrets from his subjects. Only from his girlfriend."

"I think I'll leave that one alone. I know your name is Tillie. Mine's Carmine Patti."

"You don't look Italian," she said.

"The closest I've ever been to Italy is Mulberry Street."

"Isn't that something from Dr. Seuss?"

"It's a street in New York. Little Italy."

"That where you live? New York?"

"New Jersey, actually."

"Long way to come for a funeral," said Tillie.

Patti smiled. "How come you're not with the family?"

"Bobby didn't want me to come at all. He's afraid his mother's going to cast some kind of evil spell on me."

Patti nodded toward Mendy. "Who's that, your grandfather?"

"He's a friend. His name's Mendy Pearlstein. They call him Mendy the Pearl." She giggled. "That's his gangster nickname. And he's courting my mother."

"Mendy the Pearl," Patti repeated, running it through his memory. He had never heard of Mendy the Pearl. "I guess your parents aren't together."

"The understatement of the year," said Tillie. "Right now, as we speak, my father is screwing his head off in Zurich. How's that for originality? I mean, who goes to Switzerland for sex?"

"Your mother doesn't mind?"

"My mother doesn't have a mind," said Tillie. "Just a good soul and great legs."

"What about your father?"

"He's got a mind," she said. "Sick and greedy and soaked in alcohol, but it's there. Anything else you want to know?"

"Lots, but I'd rather find out gradually," said Patti.

"How old are you?"

"Twenty-nine. Does that seem old to you?"

" 'Never trust anyone over thirty,' " said Tillie, grinning. "That gives you a year."

"Not that gradually. Let's have dinner together tonight."

"I don't do dinner. Besides, I haven't made my mind up about you yet. Tell you what, you can buy me lunch."

"What about Bobby?"

"What about him?"

"Won't he mind?"

"Lately he's been acting like a dick. He just mooches around with his big secret spread all over his face like choco-late pie. Suddenly he's John Wayne, he doesn't want to trou-ble my pretty little head. That's not the way relationships work, at least not mine."

"Are you going to want me to reveal all *my* secrets?" asked Patti, with a half smile.

"Definitely not," said Tillie. "I want you to keep them to yourself."

"How come I get an exemption?"

"Because I don't love you," said Tillie. "God, for a guy as old as you, you're dumb."

MENDY WASN'T SURPRISED when Tillie told him she'd be leaving with Carmine Patti. He had noticed them flirting in church, and on the way out to the cemetery she had asked about him. Mendy had told her that he had no idea who he was, and at the time it was true. But he knew now, thanks to Morty Klein, a Teamsters lawyer with a brown toupee, thick gray eyebrows, and an encyclopedic knowledge of the mafia.

"What's Patti doing here?" Mendy had asked him.

"Go know what these *lokshen* got with funerals," Klein said. "Don Vittorio got a hell of a turnout."

"I notice Jimmy's not here."

"Hoffa? What are you, nuts? The man's trying to get his union back, all he needs is to be consorting with known hoodlums, no offense. He sent flowers. Tea roses in the shape of a rosary. Class all the way, that's Little Jimmy. Hey, look who I see."

Mendy followed Klein's gaze to an old man wearing a well-pressed, threadbare black suit and a black stingy brim with a red feather. He was standing alone with an expression on his smooth, hard face that said he wanted to stay that way.

"Since when does he attend funerals?" asked Klein.

"Him and Vittorio go back."

"You know the guy, right? I mean personally." There was excitement in Klein's voice.

"He used to eat breakfast in my joint."

"I remember when I was a kid coming up on Hastings, he was the toughest guy in town. Everybody was scared of him."

"Yeah," said Mendy. "He was plenty tough."

Klein leaned forward and said, "Between us, you think he did that police captain from jail?"

"You're a lawyer, you know there's no limit on that."

"In other words, you think he did it?"

Mendy patted Klein on the back. "Give Jimmy my regards when you see him," he said. He walked into the crowd, mingling, and then circled around to the guy in the black suit. "Yank," he said.

"Mendy. How you feeling?"

The question made Mendy pause; it was the first time all day anyone had asked him. "Sad," he said. "Vittorio was a friend."

"Yeah," said Yank, "same here."

The two old men stood side by side in silence as Vittorio's coffin was lowered into the ground. Mendy cleared his throat and said, "How'd you get out here?"

"I took the bus."

"How about I give you a ride back?"

"You're not going to the house?"

Mendy ducked his head and said, "Nah, there's nobody there I want to see. Besides, this is an opportunity. I got a situation maybe you could give me some advice about."

"I hope it ain't of a criminal nature," said the old man. "According to the terms of my parole I ain't allowed to discuss nothing of a criminal nature."

"Aw," said Mendy. Then he looked into the old man's cold, clear blue eyes and saw they were smiling. "Tell me, you know how to find Nobody?"

"Nobody Nussbaum? Yeah, he's living with his daughter out in Birmingham."

"You think he's available?"

"He's been available since 1959," said Yank. "You want somebody tailed?"

"Yeah," said Mendy. "I think it might be wise."

Chapter Twenty-one

IN ALL THE years the don had lived in the compound at the end of the cul-de-sac there had never been so many cars parked in front, so many people crowded inside the main house. The staid Protestant neighbors watched the activity from inside their gated mansions and told one another that this was the inevitable result of allowing foreigners to move into Grosse Pointe.

The public reception was Catello's idea; he wanted the world to see that he was the new master of the House of Tucci. Uniformed attendants parked the cars. Johnny Baldini prepared mountains of canapés and sweets. There were two bars stocked with the finest liquors and wines. Verdi played softly in the background, drowned out by the din of a hundred conversations. When the delegates from the Families went back home, they would report that Luigi Catello had started out on the right foot.

Catello passed among the crowd, shaking hands and greeting the mourners with subdued affability. When he came to Annette Tucci he said, "I'm glad you're here. We need to talk."

"You're glad I'm here," she repeated in a voice loud enough to turn nearby heads. "This is my father-in-law's house, you fat fuck. It belongs to my son, Bobby, now. Who in the hell are you, telling me you're glad I'm here?"

Catello turned to Tommy Niccola and said, "A scene don't do nobody no good."

The Neck grunted his assent and put a restraining hand on his daughter's arm. "Catello's right," he said. "We talk in private. There's people here might be looking to hurt the Family."

Catello saw that a few words from Annette's father were enough to calm her. He also registered the Neck's proprietary tone. Chicago imperialism would develop into a problem, unless he could talk sense to Annette. Tomorrow Judge Barbera would be reading the will. He wanted an understanding with her before that.

Catello took a deep breath. "We could go into the don's office right now."

"Okay," said Annette. "Daddy?"

"You two go," said Tommy the Neck. "This is Tucci Family business. It don't concern me."

Annette gave her father a look of sheer adoration. By

sending her in alone with Catello he was trusting her with his cherished Center Cut.

"You're sure?" Catello asked the Neck.

"A hundred percent," Tommy said. "You sit down with Annette, you're the one's gonna need help, not her."

Annette kept her shoulders straight as she followed Catello down the hallway to the don's old study. There were tears of pride in her hard brown eyes. Never in her life had she felt more like a Niccola.

Annette hadn't been in the don's office since the day she talked to him about Bobby, but except for the absence of cigar smoke and Frank Sinatra it seemed exactly the same. When Catello sat down behind the huge mahogany desk she scowled and said, "What's this supposed to be? Like when they make some kid mayor for a day?"

"I don't want to swap insults," Catello said.

Annette gave him a contemptuous look and said, "When Al Relli gets back, he's going to knock your fat ass right off that chair, gnocchi-head."

Catello gave it an extra beat and said, "Al Relli's not coming back."

"Bullshit. I got a telegram from him this morning. From Palermo."

"'Stay strong, babe, big Al is on the way'? That one?"

"Where did *you* read it?"

"I didn't read it, I wrote it. I sent it. Relli's dead as a fuckin' doornail, may he rest in peace." He lowered his eyes for a moment and said, "I guess Bobby didn't tell you."

Annette shook her head. For once she seemed baffled and deflated. "What's Bobby got to do with it?"

"He was right there when Relli got it," said Catello. "On the walk-through for the Hoffa job. Maybe he didn't want to worry you."

Annette snorted. "The day that little prick thinks about anyone but himself, that'll be the day. Who whacked Relli?"

Catello noted the "Relli." No more Big Al. He almost felt sorry for the guy. "Bertoia. And Relli did him back before he croaked. What gets me is, why? Those two, they were like brothers. They were blood."

"Blood doesn't always mean so much," said Annette. "It's thicker than water, big deal. You ever hear anybody say blood's thicker than money?"

Catello shook his head. "You and me, we got a pie here," he said. "We divide it up into two, we each get a nice big piece. We fight over it, it could wind up on the floor. You with me so far?"

Annette nodded and tapped her fingers impatiently. "You want to cut the pie."

Catello said, "Look, I'm going to play with my cards face up. We gotta be straight with each other, hard as that might be. Otherwise this whole deal"—he gestured around the study—"is gonna eat us up, just like it did Relli."

"You said Bertoia did Relli."

"Yeah, but why? I gotta come to just one conclusion. Bobby."

"Bobby? Get serious."

"You know who he's been hangin' out with?" Catello asked.

"Yeah, Blind Willie somebody and Deaf Rufus somebody else and every other old spade with a guitar and a pair of shades in the metro area."

"You ever hear of Mendy Pearlstein?"

"Sure, he was a friend of Roberto's and the old man's," said Annette. "Mendy the Pearl. He used to be some kind of second-rater."

"He was at the funeral today."

"So? I just got done saying he was a friend of the old man's."

"With Bobby's girlfriend. They rode out to the cemetery together."

"Yeah?"

"Her and Bobby have been hanging around with the Pearl for months now. They went clubbing together, even, at the Riverboat."

"Bobby and the Pearl?"

"From what I can see, the don put them together. The question is, why? I couldn't figure it until Relli got hit. See, Relli goes down, you go down with him. I'm next in line. Then I go down, who's left?"

"Bobby? You're crazy. He's a little boy, afraid of his shadow. He can't even swallow his food in front of me."

"Pearlstein's not a little boy," said Catello.

"Pearlstein's a nothing. Where does he get the balls to go

up against a guy like Relli? And anyway, what business is it of his?"

Catello opened the don's top desk drawer, extracted a piece of paper, and slid it across the desk. "Tomorrow Judge Barbera's reading the will. Here's who's invited."

Annette squinted at the names: Roberto Tucci, Jr., Annette Niccola Tucci, Monsignor Frank DeLucca (representing the Archdiocese of Detroit), Luigi Catello, Alberto Relli, and Mendy Pearlstein.

"The old man probably left him a gold watch or something," said Annette.

"There's a power play going on right here, in front of our eyes," said Catello. "Pearlstein's helping Bobby take over the Family. That's why the don told the Commission that whoever whacked Hoffa's the new boss. Bobby's the only one who knows the plan. Pearlstein does the job, gives the credit to him, and bingo, you got the old Jew sitting next to the throne whispering in Don Bobby's ear."

Annette bit her lip in concentration. "Let's say you're right. Bobby takes over, you're out, I see that. But I'm not out, I'm in. I'm his mother. So fuck you."

"Uh-uh," said Catello. "I drop a dime to Hoffa, the hit's off. Maybe he even goes after Bobby. Either way, the Commission's gotta send in their own guys to do the job. Once they get their nose in here, Detroit ain't gonna be Tucci territory no more . . . Mrs. Tucci."

"Maybe," said Annette.

"Hey, don't take my word for it, go ask Carmine Patti."

"Who?"

"He's here to oversee the job for the Commission. Ask him what happens if the Tuccis don't fulfill the terms of the contract."

"Since when did the Commission get so powerful?" asked Annette.

"Since we got weak. We get strong again, they go away. But we don't get strong if we fight each other. You ever hear of Benjamin Franklin?"

"What's he got to do with anything?"

"He said, 'We gotta hang together, otherwise we hang separate.' In other words, cooperate."

Annette said, "What kind of cooperation are you looking for?"

Catello paused, letting the gravity of the moment ripen. "I'm ready to split with you," he said. "The legal stuff, the street business, the whole shot."

"Fifty-fifty?"

Catello shook his head. "Seventy-thirty. I know where everything is, which means I can do without you. You can't do without me. That's why I get the biggest piece."

"If you could do without me, we wouldn't be having this talk," said Annette. "What do you want?"

"You gotta promise to keep Chicago out of Detroit. And I need some information from Bobby. He's the only one who knows the whole plan for the Hoffa hit. I get that, I can do the job. You ask Bobby, he'll tell you."

"What if he doesn't?"

"I shake it out of him," Catello said. "I won't use more muscle than I need, that I guarantee."

Annette said, "How much money are we talking about here?"

"The street action alone is around a hundred million a year, and that's during the recession. The legal stuff is maybe half that. Your share would come to maybe forty-five million a year."

"I want sixty," said Annette.

"That's—"

"Forty percent."

Catello shook his head. "Forty points is too much."

Annette leaned forward and said, "You're asking me to maybe give up my own kid, you little cockroach. You think I'd do that for a lousy third?"

"When it's over, I want Bobby out of town, for good," said Catello. "You can make whatever financial arrangements for him you want, but he can't be hanging around Detroit. Agreed?"

Annette nodded. "Yeah, agreed."

"And Mendy the Pearl gets whacked."

Annette shrugged. Mendy Pearlstein was of no interest to her.

Catello sat back in the don's chair. This had been easier than he imagined. "Okay, then, we got a deal. You got your forty percent. From now on we're partners."

"Partners," said Annette. Then she surprised Catello by smiling warmly. "I'll tell you something, since we're partners. A lot of bad words have passed between us over the years, but I've always admired the way you do business. You're a smart guy, and I like smart."

"Thanks," said Catello. She had never smiled at him before, and he was genuinely pleased. Annette Tucci was a sexy broad, no two ways.

"We should celebrate," she said. "Raise a glass. You like fish?"

"Hey, what dago don't like fish?"

Annette laughed. "After the Hoffa hit, let's get together at my place and I'll make you a fish dinner you won't forget."

Chapter Twenty-two

WHEN BOBBY AND Mendy arrived at Judge Anthony Barbera's office in the Fisher Building, the others were already waiting. "Sorry we're late," said Mendy, doffing his fedora and settling into one of the padded leather chairs around the long conference table. They were late because Bobby had spent a sleepless night on Mendy's sofa, finally dozed off around six, and then refused to wake up. He wore yesterday's rumpled suit and a dazed, red-eyed expression.

Barbera, a former three-term congressman and retired recorders-court judge, was an impressive man with a mane of white hair, a pair of reading glasses perched on his prominent nose, and a look of absolute probity not matched by his career in the legislature or on the bench. He had known Mendy for forty years. Bobby he had never seen before.

The judge had a reel of film and a stack of documents in front of him. "This is the original will with a copy for each of you," he said, tapping the papers. "It was drawn by me in May of this year and signed in the presence of my secretary and a notary. Does anyone know of a subsequent will?"

The people around the table—Mendy and Bobby, Annette, Catello, and Monsignor DeLucca—all shook their heads.

"I understand Mr. Relli is away?"

Catello nodded. "On business."

At the mention of Relli's name Bobby's mouth twitched. He looked at Mendy, who pursed his lips and winked reassuringly.

"In that case," said the judge, "we can begin. All of you here know that Vittorio Tucci was an extraordinary man. He liked to run things personally, and this meeting is no exception. He made this film"—he held up the reel—"just a week before he entered his fatal coma. In it he explains his bequests in his inimitable style."

The judge put the film into the projector, switched it on, and sat back to watch with the others as the ruined face of Vittorio Tucci flashed onto the screen.

"Since you're watchin' this, that means I already croaked," Tucci said in a surprisingly strong voice. "Don't worry, it's gonna happen to you, too.

"I got some things to give away, starting with Frank DeLucca. I'm leaving the compound and all the furnishings to the church. Turn it into a convent or a monastery, whatever. The main thing is, I want Catholics crawling all over

Grosse Pointe. Also, I'm leaving you my farm in Washtenaw County. Make it a camp for colored kids, see how the hillbillies up there like that."

Tucci laughed and coughed violently into his handkerchief, inspected the contents, and said, "Remind the archbishop he promised to get every priest and nun in Detroit praying for me. I can see you from here, so no cheating. Okay, that's it for you, Frank, you can leave. You don't wanna hear the rest."

Barbera stopped the projector, handed DeLucca a copy of the will, and said, "If you have any questions, feel free to contact me. Now, if you'll excuse us—"

"I can't wait to tell the archbishop about this," the priest said. "A movie from purgatory."

"He should be so lucky," Annette muttered as the priest left.

Barbera restarted the projector, and Vittorio Tucci reappeared. "Now we get down to brass tacks," he said. "First, I'm asking Judge Barbera to set up the Roberto Tucci Foundation, to which I'm leaving the Tucci Building and all the assets of the Tucci Corporation and the subsidiaries. Barbera's got the list. The trustees of the foundation will be him, my grandson, Roberto junior, and Mendy Pearlstein. Do whatever you want with the money. What do I care? I'm dead." Tucci burst into a paroxysm of laughter that quickly became violent coughing.

Catello looked around the room. Annette was scowling, Mendy blinking back his disbelief. Bobby seemed even paler and more disoriented than before. Only Catello remained un-moved. As far as he was concerned, the old bastard could divvy things up any way he wanted—it was only a movie. The real division of spoils would take place in this world, not the next one.

On the screen Tucci said, "As far as personal gifts go, Bobby, you already got yours, and I hope you hang on to it. You want my advice, don't work too hard, that's what killed your old man. Take life easy and be an American.

"Mendy the Pearl don't get a cent, 'cause he don't appre-ciate money. You coulda been rich, you dumb Jew, all you hadda do was talk to Greenberg, we could have fixed the '45 Series." A brief smile lit Tucci's face, and Mendy grinned back at the screen. "Go to the house before the archbishop gets his hands on it and grab anything you want from the old days, mementos like. And take one of my cars; that Ply-mouth of yours is a piece of junk. That's it, boychick. *Zei gezunt.*

"I got a few other small gifts," Tucci continued. "A hun-dred thousand each to Carlo Seluchi and to Doc Florio, pro-viding I died with a smile on my face. The same to Chef Baldini plus a letter of recommendation. Fifty grand to each of the sisters and tickets back to Sicily.

"Okay, now we come to the point. Who's gonna take over the Family? I already informed the National Commission that I'm goin' with Relli. Catello, you're a good consigliere, but you ain't cut out to be a don. I never shoulda let you talk me into that Mossi thing."

Catello snorted. "Say hello to Don Alberto Relli in hell, you old bastard," he thought to himself.

"Relli, I'm leaving you my Family," said Tucci. "I got just one piece of advice for you—the future's in the suburbs.

"Last but not least, I come to my daughter-in-law, Annette Niccola Tucci. This is for you." Tucci flashed a mirthless grin and opened his phlegm-stained hankie for a long close-up. Then the screen went blank.

"Yeah, well this is for you, you toothless old cocksucker," said Annette, extending her middle finger at the screen. "Come on, Bobby, drive me home."

"I don't have my car here," he said.

"We'll take mine," said Annette, tossing him her keys. "You can grab a cab from my place."

Mendy said, "Go ahead, I'll meet you back at the joint."

YOU AND PEARLSTEIN are thick as thieves," said Annette. They were heading down Woodward Avenue toward the river. The expressway would have been faster, but Annette preferred surface streets. It was a thing she had learned from her father; there were no business opportunities on the freeway. "You gotta watch out for people like him, they glom on to money. How much did your grandfather leave you?"

"Not much, just some savings bonds and stuff," said Bobby. His eyes itched.

Annette glanced at her son. She wondered how a kid with such good bloodlines could be such a terrible liar. He was his father's boy, weak and unmanly. She wouldn't miss him when he was gone.

"I know Al Relli's dead," she said.

Bobby's fingers tightened around the steering wheel of his mother's T-Bird.

"And I know you were there when it happened. What'd you think, you were going to keep it a secret from me?"

"Yeah, since when do we have secrets," Bobby muttered.

"Open your smart mouth to me and I'll slap it shut," said Annette. "What the hell were you doing in that warehouse?"

"He wanted me to help him pick out a sound system for his car. Something that would do justice to Dean Martin."

"And then what happened?"

"I dunno. Bertoia just started shooting at him, and he shot back."

"Nobody said anything?"

"Not that I heard. I was scared shitless, I can tell you that."

"I'm not surprised," said Annette; she didn't sound sympathetic. "What about the Hoffa walk-through?"

"I don't want to talk about it," said Bobby. "As far as I'm concerned, I wasn't there and it never happened. Okay?"

"No, it's not okay. I want to know the plan."

"I forget," said Bobby stubbornly.

"There's some men in town who'll help you remember," said Annette. "Telling me will be a lot easier."

"You're really something," said Bobby.

"Why? Because I want to save you a beating? You should be grateful, you little shit."

Bobby swerved to the curb in front of the Fox Theater, brought the T-Bird to an abrupt stop, and opened the door. Half a dozen downtown people stood at a nearby bus stop. "Drive yourself home," he said, stepping out.

"You get back in here," barked Annette.

"No," said Bobby. He had never directly defied his mother before.

"Get back in here!"

"Fuck you!" Bobby screamed.

A heavyset black woman in a white nurse's uniform shook her head in dismay.

Annette sprang from the car. Red-faced with fury, she stalked to the driver's side and climbed in.

"Fuck you!" Bobby screamed again. The nurse shook her head again, but the rest of the crowd whoo-whooed and knee-slapped.

Suddenly Bobby caught himself, stared at his mother in disbelief, and bolted across Woodward. The crowd exchanged appreciative high fives and broad smiles. Say what you want about downtown Detroit, it was still a place you could see white folks acting the fool right in the middle of the street on a hot summer day.

IT WAS ABOUT noon when Tillie reached her parents' house in Bloomfield Hills. As soon as she arrived she announced that she had a stomachache. Ann Tillman poured her a cup of Earl Grey and regarded her with concern.

"I wouldn't have asked you to come if it weren't important," she said. "I have some news I'm afraid may upset you, and I want you to hear it from me, face-to-face. Your father and I are getting a divorce."

Tillie felt the muscles of her stomach relax, and she laughed. "That's all? Jesus, Mom, you scared me to death."

"We've been married for twenty-three years."

"Even murderers get out after twenty."

"You know, Mendy said something just like that. He said, 'You're a lucky broad, you done a life sentence and you're walkin' at a young age.' Not that I'm young, but I feel young, I really do."

"You're not leaving Daddy for Mendy?"

Ann laughed. "For Mendy? Mendy's a wonderful friend, but he's not interested in a serious relationship."

"*He's* not interested? Mother!"

"Don't be such a snob, Tillie. After all, you're the one who introduced us."

"I'm not a snob, it's just that he's so old. And he's a gangster."

"He doesn't seem so old to me. And as for him being a gangster, he has ten times more character than the men I know. Your father's a gentleman, and look what a shit he is."

Tillie giggled. "I can't believe I'm hearing right. I've wanted to say that to you since I was fourteen."

"You think I needed you to tell me?"

"Why now?" asked Tillie. "I mean, if you've felt this way for so long?"

"Why not now? You're grown up. There's no reason I shouldn't get on with things."

"Where will you live?"

"Right here," said Ann serenely.

"Daddy's going to let you keep the house?"

"And the place at the lake," said Tillie. "And our duplex in New York."

"We have a duplex in New York? I didn't know that."

"Neither did I, until recently," said Ann. "I understand it's just around the corner from Sotheby's. Feel free to use it anytime, there's loads of room."

"Daddy's just giving all this to you?"

Ann nodded.

"Why? He doesn't have a generous bone in his body."

"No," Ann agreed. "But this is more a matter of self-interest on his part. You might even say self-preservation. It appears that your father's been having an affair with Harley Malcolm's daughter. She's much younger than he, of course, and married, but I must say they make a photogenic couple."

"You've got pictures?"

"And a film. It's quite something."

"You put *detectives* on Daddy? That's so not you."

"Mendy arranged it. Apparently this particular detective owed him a favor."

"I bet Daddy freaked," said Tillie.

"Yes," said Ann. "Harley's the bank's biggest depositor, it seems. That's why your father decided to be so generous."

"So you get the house and the apartment, and he takes the film?"

"It seems a fair arrangement," said Ann. "Of course I'll have an extra copy. For a rainy day."

Tillie stared at her. "What have you done with my real mother?"

Ann laughed and said, "I don't know what you mean."

"Ann Tillman is a goldfish. You've turned into a shark."

"Yes," said Ann, with a laugh. "It seems that I have. Isn't it marvelous?"

Chapter Twenty-three

MENDY WAS ALONE in Vittorio Tucci's living room, inspecting photos in silver frames, when a well-built young man with an intense expression walked in. "Hi," he said, "My name's Mouse. I work for Catello."

Mendy extended his right hand. "Mendy Pearlstein," he said.

Mouse raised his own right, in which he held a Smith & Wesson .38 with a silencer. "Lean up against the wall," he said.

"Hey, buddy, I got permission," said Mendy. "Vittorio left me his keepsakes."

Mouse ran his hands over Mendy's back and under his arms, looking for a weapon. "I'm taking you for a ride," he said. The sentence, which he had practiced all day, came out smooth and professional.

"You're making a mistake," said Mendy calmly. "Call Catello, he'll tell you."

"Catello's who sent me," Mouse said. He handcuffed Mendy and prodded him with the pistol, leading him out the back door and into the passenger side of a black Lincoln. Then he drove down to the gatehouse, waved to the guard, and eased into the sweltering Grosse Pointe afternoon.

"I'm taking you to a place in Waterford," Mouse said. "When we get there, you're gonna call Bobby Tucci and tell him to meet you. Once he shows up, you're off the hook. Simple as that."

Mendy said nothing. After a long silence Mouse cleared his throat. "If you got any questions—"

Mendy remained silent, his expression mild and calm, like a man out for a pleasant Sunday ride. Mouse cleared his throat again and said, "Nobody's gonna hurt Bobby. I just need to talk to him. Understand?"

Mendy nodded.

"Jesus, say something, will ya? You're givin' me the creeps."

"I don't wanna make you nervous," said Mendy.

Mouse forced a laugh. "I got the gun, you're sittin' here in cuffs, and you don't wanna make *me* nervous? What are you, senile?"

"Aw," said Mendy. "I can tell you ain't had much experience is all."

"Don't worry about me."

"I'm worried about *me*," said Mendy. "Get a new guy jumpy, there's no telling what he's gonna do."

"I'm not jumpy," said Mouse. "And I'm not new, either."

"I'm just goin' by what I see," said Mendy in a conciliatory tone. "You want me to give you a ferinstance?"

"Go ahead."

"Okay, ferinstance, you didn't frisk me the right way. You forgot to pat down my lower legs. I could have an ankle holster."

A look of alarm crossed Mouse's face. He pulled up the cuffs of Mendy's trousers, revealing nothing more than thick ankles encased in calf-high black silk socks. "Very funny," he said.

"Another ferinstance is the cuffs," said Mendy. "You didn't lock 'em right. Look." He twisted his hands, and the right one slipped free.

"Hey," said Mouse, tightening his grip on the .38.

"Relax," said Mendy. "I ain't goin' anywhere." He slipped his hand back into the cuff. "Another giveaway is how you said, 'I'm takin' you for a ride,' back at the house—it sounded like a line from a George Raft picture. And mentioning Catello's name, that gives me information I don't already have. Plus I shouldn't be sitting in front unless you need me up here to give directions. And—"

"Okay, I get the point, shut the fuck up," said Mouse, waving his pistol. "I been with the Tuccis for three years, for your information."

"Sure, if you say so."

"When Catello takes over I'm the new consigliere."

Mendy shook his head. "You gotta be a made man to be consigliere."

"What makes you think I'm not?"

Mendy said, "Kid, I been doin' this all my life. You're a virgin. It sticks out."

"Maybe I'll lose my virginity on you," said Mouse. Now that he said it, it seemed like a good idea, sort of practice for Hoffa. Once Bobby got to the house in Waterford, Catello wouldn't give a shit what happened to the old man.

"Nah," said Mendy. "Killing me won't count."

"What do you mean it won't count?"

"To make your bones you gotta do somebody on a contract from your don."

"I never heard that."

"Hey, if all you hadda do is whack somebody, that guy on the tower down in Texas would be a made man. Think about it."

"So, I get Catello to give me the go-ahead before I do you."

"Catello ain't got the authority. He ain't the don."

"He will be," said Mouse.

Mendy shook his head and said gently, "It's never gonna happen. Don Vittorio named Relli. When the Commission finds out Catello killed him, they're gonna do the Hoffa job themselves. That's why Carmine Patti's in town. I seen you two sittin' together at Vittorio's funeral."

"How do you know about the Hoffa hit?"

"Do me a favor, put the gun down before you shoot me," said Mendy. "I can't concentrate."

"Sorry," said Mouse distractedly. He laid the pistol on his lap.

"You got the safety on?"

Mouse checked the safety and nodded.

"Good. You're not careful, you can shoot yourself. It happened to a friend of mine, Wilfie the Schmeckler, back during Pro'bition—"

"How do you know about the Hoffa hit?" Mouse repeated.

Mendy gave him a sincere, brown-eyed look and said, "Mouse, you're a bright fella, I can tell that about you. But the world you're livin' in right now, everybody knows more than you do. Especially your boss."

"Catello?"

"He told you to get me to call Bobby, right? Catello knows I'd never give up Vittorio Tucci's grandson. So what do you do? You gotta whack me, which sets you up for a murder-one rap. You wanna spend thirty years in the joint for killin' a guy my age? What kinda sense does that make?"

"You're not gonna call Bobby?"

Mendy shook his head. "I'd rather shoot myself. Hand me the gun, I'll do it right here."

"Why does Catello want me to whack you?"

"Keep me quiet. Plus I just got made a trustee of the Tucci Foundation. I go down, he maybe gets my job."

"Shit," said Mouse. He ran his fingers over his scalp and pounded his hand on the padded steering wheel. They drove for a couple of minutes in silence. Then he said, "I got an IQ of one fifty-two."

Mendy whistled. "That's high, huh?"

"It's the same as Al Haig's," Mouse said. "Genius is one-sixty."

"No kiddin'? See, I knew you were a smart kid."

Mouse gave Mendy a sharp look, but the expression on the old guy's face matched the sincerity in his voice. "I feel pretty stupid right now," he confessed.

"Aw," said Mendy. "Like I told you before, you're green is all. Take me. I can't even read and write, I just been around a few years. You get to be my age, you'll prob'ly be the savviest guy in the whole country."

Mouse was moved by Mendy's fatherly tone. His wise humility made Carmine Patti's crisp efficiency seem callow and Catello's cunning, cheap and grasping. "What do I do now?" he asked.

"You want my advice, you gotta change sides," said Mendy.

"Dump Catello?"

"Kid, there's a limit to loyalty."

"I do that, he'd come after me in a minute."

"Not if you go after him first."

"Me go after Catello?"

"Sure, why not? That's how you get experience. Besides, you wouldn't be alone."

Mouse said, "I dunno. I gotta think about this."

"There's a Denny's right up ahead. Pull in and we can get a cup of coffee. That's the think drink."

Mouse turned into the Denny's parking lot, unlocked Mendy's cuffs, and holstered his revolver. "You mind if I give you one more piece of advice?" said Mendy.

"Go ahead."

"I were you, I'd lock the pistol in the trunk. A lotta cops tend to stop off at Denny's, and they got tough carry laws out here."

"No sweat," said Mouse, tapping the gun under his jacket. "I got a permit."

Mendy blinked hard and swallowed but said nothing; Mouse's ego had taken a bad-enough beating for one day. He threw a fatherly arm over the younger man's shoulder and squeezed. Later he would tell Yank and some of the other old-timers about his new friend the genius who went out on a job carrying a licensed pistol.

FOR HALF AN hour they drank coffee, picked at an order of fries, and dissected the situation. Then Mendy went to the pay phone, made two calls, and came back grinning.

"Your turn," he said.

Mouse said, "Just like that? Things are moving so fast."

"This kind of works like the army," said Mendy. "You sit around all the time, and then bang, you gotta move. Not that I was in the army, but guys told me."

"I was in the navy," said Mouse. "I got a dishonorable discharge, though."

"Go make your call," said Mendy gently. "We're runnin' on a timetable."

THE PLACE IN Waterford was a boxy white shingle cottage on a small lake. It was dusty and stank of beer and oregano, domestic cigars and unchanged bedsheets. "Nice spot," Mendy said approvingly.

"The guys use it for fishing," said Mouse.

"Nobody's out here now?"

"Nope. You gotta clear it through Catello." Mouse felt a pang at the thought that he was stabbing his boss in the back. It lasted approximately two seconds.

"Okay then," said Mendy. "We wait. There a deck of cards around?"

"You don't want to play cards with me," said Mouse. "You wouldn't stand a chance. It's all probabilities, statistics."

"Aw," said Mendy, ducking his head, "ya gotta play gin while you wait, that's how it's done. What about just a penny a point? That way I won't get clobbered too bad."

Mouse shrugged. "Okay, I warned you. I don't want hard feelings afterwards."

They played gin and drank beer for two hours before they heard the sound of a car pulling into the driveway. Mendy went to the window and said, "Here's Rudy. Lemme go out, show him where to park out of sight."

"Okay, but we keep playing when you get back," said Mouse. He was down $215.

"The longer we play, the more you're gonna lose," said Mendy. "I'm cheating."

"Cheating?"

"Don't worry, I'm not gonna collect. I just like to keep in practice."

Mendy was gone for a minute or so. When he returned he was accompanied by a tall black man made even taller by four-inch platform shoes and a wide-brimmed Borsalino.

"Meet Rudy," Mendy said to Mouse. "Boss of the New Breed Purples of Oakland Avenue."

"At your service," said Rudy, touching the brim.

"Thanks for comin' out on such short notice," said Mendy. "It'll be a while before Catello gets here."

"I see you gentlemen are playing at cards," said Rudy.

"Gin rummy," said Mouse.

"How about a little tonk?"

"What's that?"

"A game of chance from the ghetto. Give me those cards and I'll teach it to you right quick."

Mouse concentrated as Rudy explained the game, which was a variant of gin rummy. After the third trial hand he said, "Okay, I got it."

"Penny a point?" asked Rudy.

"*No problemo*," said Mouse, giving Mendy a wink.

"I'll sit out awhile," Mendy said. He went into the kitchen and rummaged around until he found a box of Ritz crackers and a half-empty jar of Skippy peanut butter. He spread the Skippy with his pocketknife, placed the hors d'oeuvres on a plate, and brought them into the living room. Then he took a seat near the window where he could keep an eye out for Catello while he watched Rudy swindle Mouse at tonk.

They were in the middle of a hand when Mendy saw Catello's Cadillac pull up. There was no one with him. "Mouse, put the cuffs back on me," he said. "Rudy, you better wait in the bedroom till I give you the high sign."

When Catello walked in, he nodded and said, "Hello, Mendy."

Mendy nodded back and said, "Luigi. How about lettin' my hands loose here?"

"Where's Bobby?" Catello asked Mouse.

"Mendy won't make the call."

"Call Bobby and you can go," said Catello.

"Aw, I can't do that," said Mendy.

"We're not going to hurt the kid," said Catello. "I just need some information."

"He's a college boy," said Mendy. "All he knows is the names of rock-and-roll bands."

"Bullshit," said Mouse. "He knows the details of the Hoffa hit."

Catello's head snapped in Mouse's direction. "Shut the fuck up," he said.

"That's what this is all about?" said Mendy. "You shoulda said so back at the don's house, I woulda saved everybody the trouble."

"You know about the Hoffa job?"

"Bobby told me about it when he came back from the warehouse in Pontiac. He was pretty shook up about Relli."

"Yeah, well, accidents happen," said Catello. "Besides, Bobby had no business being there in the first place."

"That's what I told him," said Mendy. "Certain things kids gotta learn for themselves. I was the same way. I remember this one time, I musta been maybe nineteen, around in there—"

Catello held up his hand and said, "You know the details of the job?"

"It's so simple it's ridiculous," said Mendy. "Relli meets Jimmy in the parking lot of the Red Fox on Thursday at four-thirty. Jimmy follows Relli, to see some piece of property in the sticks. They get there, Relli shoots him, dumps the body, and that's that."

"Hoffa know where this property is?"

"Out Inkster Road's all I know."

"That's good enough," said Catello. "I pull up in the Red

Fox lot and I go, 'Hey, Jimmy, howya doin'? Relli's still in Sicily, he asked me to show you the property, follow me.' We pick some nice quiet place, and when we pull in, Mouse, you're waitin'. We take Hoffa, you dump the car and lose the body, and that's that."

"What makes you think Hoffa's gonna follow *you*?" asked Mendy.

Catello picked up a Ritz cracker and munched thoughtfully. Finally he said, "Me and Jimmy have history. He's got no reason to worry about me."

"What about Bobby?" asked Mouse. "You gonna let him off the hook?"

"Fuck Bobby," said Catello. "We don't need him anymore."

"Now you're talkin'," said Mendy. "How about you spring these cuffs? They're cuttin' off my circulation."

"You know better than that," said Catello. "Mouse, you want to make your bones? Tonight's the night."

"You want me to kill Mendy?"

"Hey, come on, I'm sittin' right here listenin'," said Mendy.

"Sorry," Catello said. He took Mouse aside and quietly said, "Wait till I leave, then smother him with a pillow and drop him someplace."

"Where?"

"There's a million lakes out here. Choose one."

"You do this, the Purples are gonna come after you," said Mendy.

Catello laughed and said to Mouse, "You better get mov-

ing. If he croaks from Alzheimer's, it don't count as an official hit."

"Hey, I'm serious, the Purples are back. They're all over
the place." Mendy paused, waiting, but Rudy didn't appear.
He raised his voice and called, "Even out here."

"What are you yelling about?" Catello demanded.

"Me," said Rudy, ambling out of the kitchen on his two-
tone platforms, a peanut butter and Ritz in one hand and an
Uzi in the other.

Mendy twisted his hands free and said, "Jeez, I thought
you forgot me."

"I was enjoying myself, just watching you work your
show," said Rudy. He turned to Catello and said, "I can't help
it, man, whenever I'm around this old dude he takes my
black ass clear out of the moment."

Catello gave Mouse a do-something signal with his eyes,
but Mouse simply returned a defiantly resentful glare. "You
didn't tell me it doesn't count if it's not an official contract,"
he said to Catello. "You never mentioned that."

"That's crap," Catello snapped. He was fighting to regain
his poise. Turning to Rudy he said, "Look, kid, I don't know
what kinda bullshit you been hearin', but my name is Luigi
Catello. That mean anything to you?"

Rudy shook his head. "Nope."

"You heard of the Tucci Family, right?"

"Yeah, they the I-talian mafia."

"Good. Well, I'm the head of the Tucci Family. That's who
you're fuckin' with. Now put down the gun and beat it."

"Wait a minute," said Rudy. "If you the head of the Tucci Family, how come your name ain't Tucci? What are you, some kind of brother-in-law?"

"Mouse, explain it to him," said Catello.

"He's an interloper," said Mouse. "That means—"

"I know what it means, motherfucker," said Rudy.

"He don't mean no harm," said Mendy. "He suffers from a high IQ."

"Yeah, sorry," said Mouse. "No offense."

"No damage, no foul, my man," said Rudy.

Catello said to Rudy, "Give me the gun and you can have a piece of the smack and coke action on the East Side. You'll be the richest eggplant in town."

"Nah, I'm already independently wealthy," said Rudy easily. "Besides, I got a feelin' you sellin' me wolf tickets."

"Listen to what I'm telling you—I can make you the fuckin' colored don of Detroit."

"Man, I got a problem with that don shit, on account of Don Ho." He turned to Mendy. "What we gonna do with the godfather here?"

"I been thinkin'," said Mendy. "You still got Muhammad Ali?"

Rudy's dark eyes lit up. He turned to Mouse and said, "This man, just one thought from his mind be enough to blow off the whole top of a average motherfucker's head."

"Who's Ali?" asked Mouse.

"Whatever you're getting, I'll triple it," said Catello to Rudy.

Rudy ignored the offer and said, "Ali is our mascot. He gonna love Mr. Softbody here."

"Mouse, you fuckin' wop, when this is over I'm gonna put a piece of you in every gravel pit in Michigan," said Catello. "What are you, nuts, siding with a nigger?"

"What kind of mascot?" asked Mouse. "Like a stuffed animal?"

Rudy smiled and looked directly into Catello's brown eyes. "Better not let Ali hear you call him stuffed," he said.

"He's a kangaroo," said Mendy.

"Yeah, but not no regular kangaroo. He's a pissed-off, seven-foot flying purple people-eater, that's who Ali is. And I'll tell you one other something. Delbert, this militant friend of mine? He been readin' *Elijah Speaks* to Ali until he thinks he's some kinda Muslim. Got that animal all full of race pride. So if I was you, my man, I'd just ease off on that nigger talk, 'less you want a seven-foot kangaroo dick up your pasta-fied ass."

Chapter Twenty-five

WHEN BOBBY GOT back to the apartment he found Tillie in the bedroom reading Vonnegut. "We've got to talk," he said.

"Finally," she said, closing the book.

Bobby took a deep breath and said, "The other day, when I went to Detroit I met a guy named Al Relli. He's a friend of my mother's. Was. He's dead." He paused.

"Keep going."

"He was going to kill Jimmy Hoffa. And I was supposed to tag along as an apprentice hit man sort of. Only he got numbed in a shoot-out in a warehouse in Pontiac."

"Where were you?"

"Right there. Ten feet away, maybe. I could smell the gunpowder or whatever it is. I can still smell it."

"Jesus," said Tillie.

"I panicked. For a while I just drove around. Then I went to Mendy's."

Tillie threw her book at Bobby. "I can't believe all this was happening to you and you didn't say a thing to me," she said.

"I didn't, you know, want to get you more involved than you had to be."

"I feel like I don't know you at all. You were actually going to kill Jimmy Hoffa?"

"Are you kidding? I was going to get out of it, convince Relli I was weird."

"Jesus, no wonder you were freaked out the other day," said Tillie. "Well, since this Relli guy's dead, it's all over. No?"

"I wish it was. Mendy heard from one of his cronies that some mafia honcho was sent in to make sure the Hoffa job gets done."

"Sent in? From where?"

"New Jersey," said Bobby. "What difference does that make?"

Tillie was silent for a long moment. Then she looked directly into Bobby's eyes and said, "I think I met this guy at your grandfather's funeral. Is his name Carmine Patti?"

Bobby nodded.

"Oh, shit," said Tillie. She was grinning.

"What?"

"He tried to hit on me."

"And?"

"I was tempted. The way you've been acting."

Bobby surprised her by smiling back. "I sure pissed you off," he said.

"You sure did."

"How do I get back on your good side?"

"Try communicating for a change."

"Isn't there an easier way?" Tillie stared at him, and Bobby said, "Hey, I'm only kidding."

"I know when you're kidding," said Tillie. She sighed. "I don't feel like being mad at you right now. Not when you're in this kind of trouble."

"Don't worry, I can handle things."

"Patti is a dangerous guy."

"Yeah? Well, I'm a pretty dangerous guy myself. Not." He laughed, and Tillie did too.

"When you're like this, you *are* dangerous," she said.

THE ELEVATOR OPENED and Annette stepped into her father's stubby embrace. "How's things in the Motor City?" he asked.

"I came to talk," said Annette. "Not on the phone."

"So let's talk."

"I gotta freshen up first," she said.

Annette went upstairs, put on her mother's black silk dressing gown and a pair of satin slippers, and touched her neck with My Sin. Her father whistled when she came into the den. "You're a beautiful woman," he said appreciatively.

"As beautiful as she was?"

"Your mother, rest her soul, never had your inner beauty," said Tommy the Neck. He poured them each a glass of Chianti and raised his in a toast. "To my little girl."

She raised her own glass and said, "To the Center Cut."

Tommy sat down next to her on the leather couch. "So, what's so important?" he asked.

"Everybody's missing," she said.

"Who's everybody?"

"Catello, for one. I haven't seen him since the day before yesterday when they read the will. Nobody knows where he is. And Bobby's gone, too. I think they might be off together, planning something."

"Bobby doesn't have the balls," said Tommy.

"Maybe he does. He hasn't been himself lately. Or it could be that Catello's got him."

Tommy stroked his chin, contemplating the situation in all its complexity. Finally he said, "We gotta do the job on Hoffa before Catello. You already know most of the details from Relli. What you don't have is the time. Maybe Catello got that from Bobby, maybe not. But we don't need it."

"What do you mean?" asked Annette.

"Call Hoffa's office, tell his secretary Al Relli's stuck in Sicily. He wants you to go to the meet instead of him, 'cause it's a deal that won't wait. Say that you gotta reschedule, move it up. Let Hoffa pick the new time and place. He won't be scared of you, just make sure he knows you're coming alone."

"What if Catello calls him, too?"

"Don't worry. I'll get word to Jimmy that Catello's out," said Tommy. "That this is strictly your deal and Relli's."

"Okay, I meet Hoffa, I'm alone. Then what?"

"Tell him you wanna take one car, you can talk on the way. Try to make it yours, but don't insist. Drive him out in the country, we choose the spot in advance. When you get there, take him."

"Me?"

"Why the hell not?" said Tommy. "You can handle a gun as good as any guy. Just give him one to the head, and bye-bye, Jimmy."

Annette stared at her father. "Do you really mean it?"

"Don't make me repeat myself. After you do him, stick him in a body bag," said Tommy. "He's a little guy, but it's dead weight, so you're gonna have to tug. Close up the bag and wait, Ralph and Jo-Jo will come by. I'm sending them to Detroit to dispose of the body, but I don't want them to know who they're disposing of."

"Ralph and Jo-Jo are blood," said Annette.

"Yeah, but there's gonna be heat on this you wouldn't be-lieve," said Tommy. "The only two people in the world I trust a hundred percent are sitting in this room."

Annette sat in silence for what seemed like a long time. Her father was sending her, a woman, out to make her bones in the biggest hit of the century. "I don't know what to say," she mumbled.

Tommy shrugged his neckless shoulders. "You earned it," he said simply.

"I won't let you down," Annette said.

"I got all the confidence in you," said Tommy. "Now, remember, you're gonna be the last person they know of who saw Hoffa, so naturally the first finger's gonna point at you. But if there's no body, there's no crime, that's the law. You dropped him back off at the Red Fox. For all you know he skipped the country with Teamster money, or he's holed up with a broad somewhere. Maybe they believe you, maybe not. But they can't do a thing if they ain't got the body."

"There's half a dozen places I can think of to ditch him," said Annette.

"If you can think of 'em, so can they. Every cop in America's gonna be looking to get famous finding Jimmy Hoffa. We gotta put him where nobody'd ever even dream of looking."

"Like where?"

Tommy grinned widely, exposing his yellow, nubby teeth, and said, "I got an idea." He crooked his finger and leaned over to whisper his secret in her ear. She bent toward him, but at the last moment she turned her head so that her face met his. "Oh, Daddy," she breathed and opened her lips.

Chapter
Twenty-
six

MENDY AND MOUSE were at the Bull Pen eating steak and eggs when the phone rang. It was Rudy. "Excuse the interruption," he said, "but you think you could swing by here?"

"Something the matter?" asked Mendy.

"Definitely," said Rudy. "Something is definitely the matter."

Rudy was waiting outside the clubhouse when they arrived. Mouse took a look at the sign and said, "The Toussaint l'Ouverture Freedom Alliance of Oakland Avenue?"

"That's our new name," said Rudy apologetically. "The lady from the Ford Foundation said it sounds more militant. They some badass hard-liners over there. But don't worry, we still New Breed Purples when the foundation people ain't around."

"Hey, you gotta go with what works," said Mendy. "I remember when Lefty Levine opened up a gambling joint called the Theodor Herzl Hebrew Aid Society just down the block here. He hired a rabbi to stand out in front like a cigar store Indian. So, what's the problem?"

"Y'all better see this for yourselves," said Rudy. He unlocked the door and led them inside. The place was empty except for a noticeably subdued Delbert, who sat at his desk in the front.

"Hiya, Delbert," said Mendy.

Rudy shot Delbert a contemptuous look and said, "Catello still in my office?"

"He's back there."

"Come on, say hello," Rudy said. They followed him to the office, where Luigi Catello sat slumped in a chair, his eyes shut, his plump features twisted into a grimace.

Mouse said, "Luigi, you don't look too good."

"You gotta speak up a little," said Rudy, "him being dead and all."

Mouse stumbled, bumping into Mendy, who took him by the shoulders and guided him into a chair. Mendy inspected the body and said, "What croaked him?"

"Ask Delbert," said Rudy.

"Fear croaked his ass," said Delbert resentfully. "He supposed to be the baddest dude in the mafia. How the fuck I know he scared of animals?"

"Delbert put him down in the cellar and let Ali off the chain," said Rudy.

"The kangaroo did this?" said Mendy. "I don't see no marks."

"Ali never laid a hand on him," said Delbert. "Hell, he's a damn vegetarian, he don't bite. He wasn't gonna do nothin'."

"So what happened?" asked Mendy.

"Like I told you, the motherfucker died of fear. He just grabbed that fat chest of his and flopped on the floor."

"Jeez," said Mendy. "That's a new one."

Mouse muttered, "May God have mercy on his soul."

"Amen," said Rudy. "Now, what we gonna do with him?"

"Catello's people know he was coming to Waterford to see me. My ass is in a sling," said Mouse.

"Oh, yeah?" said Delbert with evident relief. "You hear that, Rudy? We ditch the body, nobody ain't gonna suspect us, man. It's all on this motherfucker."

Rudy said, "The Mouse ain't gonna say a word, that what you think? Not even mention us at all?"

Delbert said, "Shoot his ass and ditch 'em together."

Mouse drew his pistol and said, "Hey, you chocolate cocksucker, anybody gets shot around here it's gonna be you."

"Man, put that away, nobody's gonna shoot anybody," said Rudy. "Delbert, the Mouse come all the way over here to give us a hand, and you talkin' about what? Shoot the motherfucker?"

"Shit," said Delbert. "I told you we don't need to be gettin' mixed up with these damn dagos."

Mendy snapped his fingers and said, "Hey, did I ever tell you about Dr. Fred Marcoo?"

Mouse, Delbert, and Rudy all shook their heads.

"Back during Pro'bition, Dr. Fred Marcoo was a sawbones who used to hang out at Jew Mary's cathouse. He was a real prominent guy, but regular. Sometimes I sold him Scotch, he drank Haig & Haig. One time he took an appendix out for a cousin of mine, also named Mendy Pearlstein, I might have mentioned him."

"Man, what this got to do with the corpse?" asked Delbert.

Rudy gave Delbert an admonishing look and said, "Go on, man, tell us about Dr. Magoo."

"Marcoo. Anyways, this one day he comes in and I can see he's feelin' blue. He says, 'Mendy, today a patient of mine just keeled over and died in the middle of an examination.' I said, 'Jeez, that's tough. Whaddya do in a jam like that?' And Dr. Marcoo told me something I never forgot. He said, 'When a patient dies in your office, always drag him out in the hall and lay him down so it looks like he was on the way in to see you.' "

"Man say, 'Drag him in,'" said Rudy. "That's some deep strategy." He was grinning.

"See, Catello wasn't murdered, he's just dead," said Mendy. "Anybody could have a heart attack. The question is, who finds him, and where? Mouse, you know where Carmine Patti's stayin'?"

"At the Ponch," said Mouse. Calling the Pontchartrain Hotel by its nickname made him feel like an insider.

"Okay, give him a ring, tell him Catello's on his way down to see him about something urgent. Tell Patti to meet him in the parking garage in an hour. Then stick Catello in the trunk of your car, drive him over there. Delbert, you follow in Catello's car. When you get there put Catello behind the wheel of his Caddy, turn the radio on, wipe for prints, and you're all set."

"Let the man think Catello died on the way in to see his ass," said Rudy.

"Sure. Then he's Patti's problem," Mendy said.

"Slick," Delbert conceded.

"Thanks. Mouse, you better use a pay phone; the hotel switchboard keeps a record."

Rudy flipped Mouse a quarter. "Go up to the Gulf station on Woodward. They customer-friendly when it comes to white people."

"One thing, though," said Mouse. "If that doctor just dragged the guy out into the hall like that and washed his hands of the whole mess, how come he was so upset?"

"Oh, yeah," said Mendy. "See, it turned out that his wife had just totaled her new Buick that afternoon."

Rudy nodded. "That'll mess up a mood," he said.

Chapter Twenty-seven

ON WEDNESDAY, JULY 30, Annette Tucci awakened with a mouth full of fur. Scratch, curled up next to her, had somehow wedged the tip of his tail between her teeth. Gently she stroked the cat until he stirred. He arched his back and purred as he slid his wet tail onto the satin pillow.

Annette glanced at her clock radio—ten-thirty. At this moment she was still a mafia widow, one of many; in a few hours she would be the most powerful woman in organized crime.

She owed it all to her father. He was a giant, a genius, the greatest man she had ever known. Compared to him, Relli and Catello were little boys squabbling in a school yard. She was only glad that she could repay his love and trust by delivering Detroit into his grand scheme. Someday, many years from now she hoped, she herself would rule the Center Cut. It was the destiny of the Niccolas.

Annette rose slowly, drew a bath, soaked her lean, strong body in rose water, and toweled off in front of Scratch's hungry stare. Wrapped in white terrycloth, a violet turban on her head, she watched the sailboats on Lake St. Clair as she ate half a Fruit-of-the-Month Club honeydew and sipped specially roasted Colombian coffee.

Three cups later, Annette went to her dressing room and chose a conservative black silk suit, a white blouse that came to her neck, and sensible shoes. She wore light makeup, and her only jewelry was a small gold necklace that had belonged to her mother. When she inspected herself, she saw an attractive, unspectacular woman. It was a look designed to put the priggish Hoffa at ease.

Next, Annette loaded her purse, a small black custom-made Gucci given to her by her cousins Ralph and Jo-Jo, who had flown in from Chicago the night before. The Gucci had a special pistol mount that allowed her to aim and fire without taking the gun from the purse. She also packed two Ziploc bags, a tube of lip gloss, a roll of sugarless wintergreen mints, a small jar of hand cream, and a butcher knife. Then she snapped the purse shut, kissed Scratch on the nose, and walked out of the house ready to make history.

THERE HAD BEEN nobody waiting for Carmine Patti this time when he arrived at Metro Airport, nor had he expected anyone. He had only been gone six hours, after all, just long enough to fly into Newark Airport and confer with the five old men of the Commission in a private room at La Luna Restaurant in Paramus.

Two of them, Edward "the Judge" Polumba and the notoriously taciturn Sam Spadollini, headed New York Families. The others were Alfredo Orellini of Providence, representing all of New England; Michael "the Actor" DiBlanca of Los Angeles; and Willie "Knuckles" Bontera from Dallas. Into their hands had been entrusted the executive decision-making of the American underworld.

"I wouldn't have requested such an urgent meeting, but the situation in Detroit requires a decision," Patti had said, with a formality appropriate to the occasion. "Frankly, I have no idea what to do."

The Commissioners nodded in approbation; humility in a young man was a prized, and increasingly rare, quality. "Speak freely," said Don Polumba.

"These Detroit people are crazy," said Patti. "They've killed each other off. First Don Tucci—all right, that could have been a natural death. Then Relli gets shot in a warehouse by his cousin. At the funeral, Catello tells me he's in charge. Three days later he turns up dead in his car in the parking garage of my hotel. The doctors say it was a heart attack."

"But you doubt this?" said Don Polumba.

"When I found him, his car radio was tuned to a black radio station," said Patti. "From what I know of Catello, he wasn't the kind of man who listened to Curtis Mayfield." The old men nodded. Not one of them had ever heard of Curtis Mayfield. Silently they congratulated themselves on choosing this perceptive young American as their emissary.

"If Catello was murdered," said Orellini, "who did it?"

Michael DiBlanca said, "With all the respect, I don't see what difference it makes. Unless somebody here has a personal interest in the matter?" They looked at one another and shrugged. "We had a deal with Vittorio Tucci. His Family does the Hoffa contract by the end of the month. Tomorrow's the thirtieth, and Hoffa's still walking around. Which means the contract's no good. Which means we do what's necessary."

Willie Bontera cracked his knuckles for attention and said, "The Tuccis got another forty-eight hours."

"The Tuccis are all dead," said DiBlanca irritably. "Patti just said so. What're they, gonna come back from the grave to do the job?"

"Is that right?" asked Don Polumba. "Are they all dead?" As the senior member, he was the Commission's informal chairman.

"The only remaining Tuccis of any consequence are the daughter-in-law, Annette, and the grandson, Bobby," said Patti.

"A woman and a boy," said DiBlanca.

"She's the daughter of Tommy Niccola, don't forget," said Orellini.

"All the more reason to move now," said DiBlanca. "I'm

not speaking from greed. I control Los Angeles, what do I care about Detroit? But we can't allow chaos."

"No," said Bontera. "We made a promise to Vittorio Tucci. Okay, he's dead, but nobody sitting around this table is immortal. Each one of us will be in his shoes sooner or later. We don't live up to our word, nobody here will be certain his plans for the future of his Family will be respected. And then there *will* be chaos."

"Let's be practical," said Orellini. Although he had been born in Sicily, his control of New England had won him a reputation for Yankee pragmatism. "We're only talking about two days here."

"Unless the Tuccis ask for an extension," said Bontera. "They got that right."

"What Tuccis, for Christ's sake?" said DiBlanca.

"The grandson," said Bontera. "If he's interested."

"I don't think he is," said Patti. "But Annette's another story. She's ambitious for the boy."

"I still say we take over now, before a vacuum sets in," said DiBlanca.

"And I still say a promise is a promise," said Bontera.

Don Polumba looked at his fellow New Yorker. "Sam? You haven't said a word."

"Respect the deal," rasped Spadollini.

"Yes," said Polumba. "We gave our word, we must respect our word. We're not politicians here, we're Men of Honor. Carmine, go back to Detroit, speak with the mother and the boy. Explain our arrangement with Don Tucci. Give this

Bobby another two weeks. If he hits Hoffa, we back him for boss. If he's not interested, we offer a fair buyout. Something to keep Tommy the Neck quiet."

"What if Annette decides that she wants control of the Tuccis herself?"

"Impossible," said Willie Bontera. "A woman can never be the head of a Family."

"For once I agree with Willie," said DiBlanca.

"Don Tucci would have been the first to say so," Orellini said.

Don Polumba nodded. "It is the grandson or no one," he ruled.

Patti said, "If the boy doesn't want it, what about the Hoffa contract?"

"You do it."

"Me?"

"Acting for us. After which Detroit will become an open city. You will represent our interests there. That is, if you feel you are capable."

"I am honored by your faith in me," said Carmine Patti, trying to conceal his dismay. Running an open city was the most thankless job in organized crime. "But—"

Sam Spadollini cleared three months' worth of cigar phlegm from his massive lungs and raised his eyelids to half mast. "You leave us worry about the honor, kid," he rasped. "You just concentrate on not fucking up."

Don Spadollini's admonition stayed with Patti during the flight back to Detroit, and it was still ringing in his ears when he arrived at the Pontchartrain and found a message to call Annette Tucci at home. "This is a coincidence," he said when he got her on the phone. "I was going to call you tonight."

"It's time we got together," she said. Her manner was brisk and peremptory. "Meet me in the hotel bar in an hour."

Patti was on his second dry martini when Annette walked in, accompanied by a vaguely familiar, bullet-headed man with the build of a washing machine. She left him at the door, took a seat, and motioned for Patti to join her. As he approached she looked him over slowly. "Six-one?" she said.

"Six-two," Patti said with a boyish smile.

"Broad shoulders, narrow waist. You were a football player, right?"

"In the distant past," said Patti, warming up the smile and putting some twinkle in his blue eyes. "You look like you might have been a cheerleader."

"I look like a cheerleader? What are you, a moron?"

"I meant it as a compliment."

"You meant it as a come-on."

"You're the one who started with the body talk," said Patti.

"I was trying to figure out if I wanted to screw you later on," said Annette. "I don't, so let's get down to business."

"Wow, you come on strong, lady," said Patti, still smiling.

Annette leaned across the table until their faces were just inches apart. "Don't patronize me, sonny. You talk to me with respect. I'm a fucking widow."

"Sorry," said Patti.

"Okay, let's start all over," said Annette. "How was Jersey?"

"What makes you think I was in Jersey?"

"Him," said Annette, nodding toward the washing machine. Now Patti knew why the guy looked familiar. "I can tell you what you had for lunch. So, how's the Commission?"

"Nervous," said Patti.

"They can stop worrying," said Annette. She opened her purse, extracted two small Ziploc bags, and passed them to Patti. He examined them in the faint candlelight, raised his eyes to meet her steady gaze, and said, "Hoffa's?"

Annette nodded. "You know what they say—a finger's worth a thousand words."

"You giving these to me?"

"One to a customer," she said, picking up the second bag with her long red fingernails and replacing it in her purse. "Go ahead, get it printed, just to make sure."

Patti put the bag in his jacket pocket. "When did it happen?"

"This afternoon."

"Who did it?"

"I did," said Annette. "One bullet, right between the eyes."

"I don't believe you."

"What do you want me to do, bring you his head in a doggy bag?"

"Where's the body?"

Annette shook her head. "You don't need to know." The truth was that she didn't know herself.

"All right," said Patti. "Say I believe you. Now what?"

"The contract's fulfilled, right on time. That means that

Detroit stays under Tucci control. Go back and tell the Commission. I'm in charge."

Patti shook his head. "They'll never approve it. It's not fair, but there it is." To his surprise he felt sheepish. He had just come from a meeting with five of the top crime bosses in the country, and Annette Tucci had more force and charisma than any of them.

"I don't need their approval," she said.

"You know what they'll do? If you make a move like that?"

"What?"

"Declare Detroit an open city." Patti frowned and said, "Probably put me in charge."

"I do the job on Hoffa, and you take over because you've got a dick," said Annette. "You think that's how it's going to work?"

"Hey, I don't want Detroit," said Patti. "Refereeing turf fights between every Family in the country? In a shithole like this? It's the worst thing that could happen to my career."

"Then tell them no dice."

"I can't," said Patti. "I'm responsible to the Commission. Hoffa was only half the deal; finding a new boss's the other half. And it can't be you. To these older guys that would be heresy, like a woman pope."

"Yeah, that would be terrible," said Annette. "But, that's not how everybody feels. My father, for example."

"Oh?" This was something new.

"Yeah, oh. He's in my corner all the way."

"Your father's a powerful man," said Patti carefully. "But

the Commission is made up of powerful men. I'd hate to see a clash of wills. That way everyone loses."

"Yeah, but some people are gonna lose more than others," said Annette. "You know who's gonna lose big time?"

"Who?"

"The guy I decide to dig up Hoffa and rebury the corpse on his property and then drop a dime. That guy's gonna get his ass in a sling. Maybe it'll be Don Polumba. Maybe it'll be that Actor from L.A. It could be anybody."

"I don't believe you'd do that."

"Why, 'cause it's against the rules? The rules don't apply to me, remember? Besides, all this Sicilian voodoo crap is a thing of the past. This is a business, and I'm taking it over, no matter what some Mustache Petes in Jersey say. Chicago's backing me. So if the Commission wants to fight, they better bring their lunch. Is that clear?"

"Couldn't be any clearer."

"Good. Then run your cute ass back to Jersey and make it clear to the College of Cardinals."

It was a dismissal, but Patti didn't budge. "No," he said. "It's the wrong message, and I'm not going to deliver it."

"I warned you about patronizing me," said Annette.

"I'm not; I'm giving you advice, which is what I get paid to do. If I tell the Commission what you just said, there *will* be a war. Maybe you and your father can win, but I doubt it. Even if you do, the price is going to be exorbitant."

"So what's your advice, counselor?" Annette's tone was sarcastic, but Patti could tell she was interested.

"You said two things I agree with completely. First, this is a business matter. The Commission feels the same way. They're like a hands-off board of directors. They don't want to get involved in Detroit, they just want ultimate oversight. Give them that, they won't interfere."

"How?"

"By using Bobby as your front man."

Annette snorted. "What's the matter with using my father?" she asked.

"He'd scare them to death," said Patti. "There are a lot of bosses around the country who consider Don Niccola a threat. He's already got too much. Listen to me, use Bobby. It doesn't have to be permanent."

"What do you mean by that?"

"It goes back to the second thing you said. This old-country stuff can't last. As the dinosaurs die off they're going to be replaced by a generation of Americans who don't give a damn about macho taboos."

"Guys like you," said Annette.

"Exactly like me," said Patti. "When we're in control, you can step forward on your own."

Annette stared into the hazy darkness of the bar. Then she said, "I don't believe you guys are gonna be any better than the Mustache Petes, and I'm not waiting around to find out. I appreciate you don't want a war, and I value your advice. Come up with a solution that doesn't leave me in the kitchen, I'm ready to listen. But until then, I'm in charge and I intend to stay in charge."

Patti opened his hands in a gesture of resignation. "You're the boss."

"I like you when you're being obedient," said Annette. "Why don't you come to work for me? You'd make a good consigliere."

"I'm honored," said Patti, "but I'm happy where I am."

"Okay," said Annette. "I can always use a friend next to the Commission." She smiled sweetly and added, "Especially one whose prints I've got on Jimmy Hoffa's Ziploc finger bag."

Chapter Twenty-eight

MENDY OPENED THE Bull Pen at six-thirty. Ten minutes later, Klein the Teamster lawyer came in. Mendy hadn't seen him since the funeral, and he had never seen him this early in the morning.

Klein took a seat at the counter. When Mendy came over Klein lowered his voice, although no one was nearby, and said, "You hear the news?"

Mendy shook his head.

"Somebody nabbed Hoffa yesterday."

"Jeez," said Mendy. "Who'd do a thing like that?"

"What are you, kidding? Who wouldn't? The guy's got more enemies than communism. You haven't heard anything?"

"Where would I hear?"

"You were seeing a lot of the don before he croaked," said Klein. "I figured maybe he might have mentioned something."

"Aw, we went to a couple ball games," said Mendy. "Jeez, the Tigers stink this year. I'm sorry Vittorio had to go out in such a bum season. What can I get you?"

"I think I'll skip breakfast," said Klein. "I want to drop in on a couple more guys, see who knows what."

"You workin' for the Teamsters on this?" asked Mendy.

Klein stood, straightened his toupee, and clicked his dentures into place. "This is strictly freelance," he said. "It's like the schvartzes say, 'Knowledge is power, brother.' "

Mendy watched Klein's Buick head down Michigan Avenue. Then he called Bobby in Ann Arbor.

"It's not even seven," Bobby said in a thick voice. "I had a gig last night."

"Sorry, but we gotta eat salami and eggs," said Mendy. "Soon as possible."

"Salami and eggs?" said Bobby. "What are you talking about?"

"It's a code. It means I need to talk to you in person."

"It can't wait?"

"There's nothing that can't wait. The only thing is, what happens while it's waiting?"

Bobby laughed and coughed at the same time. "You into Zen now? Okay, I'll be there in an hour."

"Don't speed, drive careful," said Mendy. "And Bobby? Somebody knocks on your door, don't answer it."

Bobby and Tillie got to the Bull Pen around eight. They were red-eyed from lack of sleep and gave off the aroma of marijuana, which mingled with the diner's usual morning blend of bacon grease, brewed coffee, burnt toast, filter cigarettes, and generic aftershave.

"Salami and eggs," Bobby said in a stage whisper.

Mendy said, "Tillie, Bobby and me need to discuss something. Why don't you grab some breakfast at the counter. I got nice western omelettes today."

"We're in this together," said Tillie. Bobby nodded.

"Nah," said Mendy. "You're not in it. If Bobby wants to put you in later, that's his business."

Tillie said, "I can't burn my bra 'cause I'm not wearing one, and besides, I'm hungry. So you have your manly chat and get me when you're finished. I'll be the little lady by the jukebox with her mouth full of flapjacks."

"Jeez, I hope she ain't mad at me," said Mendy, as Tillie sauntered over to the counter.

"If she were, you'd know it," said Bobby. "What's so important?"

"Yesterday somebody snatched Jimmy Hoffa."

"I didn't hear about it on the radio," said Bobby.

"The radio don't know about it yet."

"Then how do you?"

"A guy stopped by."

"Well, we know it wasn't Relli," said Bobby. "It must have been Catello, huh?"

Mendy shook his head. "It wasn't him."

"How do you know?"

"It don't matter, I just do. So who does that leave?"

"I don't know. Who?"

"Your mother or Carmine Patti. Those are the only ones I can figure."

Bobby scowled. "What do I care who did it? I don't give a shit if Hoffa got abducted by Martians, it's got nothing to do with me."

Mendy pressed his lips together and widened his eyes. "Patti called me this morning. He wants to sit down. He should be here any time. In fact, here he is now."

Bobby saw Carmine Patti walk in, looking crisp and fresh in a white linen suit. "Asshole," he said. "He hit on Tillie."

"Let him do the talking," said Mendy. "And keep the personal stuff out of it."

Patti saw Tillie at the counter and did a small double take. "This is a surprise," he said.

"Surprise? I've been sitting here waiting for you since seven. Don't tell me you forgot our date." She waited for the confusion to spread over his face before saying, "Relax, I'm here with Bobby."

"Does he know about us?"

"What's to know?"

Patti pulled his face together as he walked toward Bobby and Mendy. "We haven't really met," he said, extending his hand. Mendy gave it a shake. Bobby put his hands in the pockets of his jeans.

"Coffee?" said Mendy.

"Black. I'd like to talk to Bobby alone, if you don't mind."

"No way," Bobby said. "Either you say what you want to say in front of Mendy or skip it."

"I'm sorry you feel that way," said Patti. "No offense to Mendy, but this is just between us."

"Hey, I got a joint to run," said Mendy to Bobby. "You and me can talk later. I'll send one of the girls over with the coffee."

"Quite a character," said Patti. "A real old-timer. Listen, Bobby, I came to talk to you about your family."

"You got balls," said Bobby. "As you would say."

"I'm just doing my job," Patti said. "Back east some very important men are going to ask me who's taking over the Tucci Family business. What do I tell them?"

Bobby shrugged. "Tell them whatever you want; it's got nothing to do with me."

"Yes, it does. Your grandfather named Alberto Relli to succeed him, but we both know that won't happen. The same goes for Catello. You've got the strongest claim now; after all, you're the last Tucci."

"The last Tucci," said Bobby. "Sounds like an anthro course. Aren't you forgetting the ever popular Annette Niccola Tucci?"

"I've spoken to her. Frankly she wants to run things herself."

"Fine with me."

"It can't happen. The men I work for won't accept it. It's either you or the Commission takes over. Personally I'm hoping it will be you."

"What do you care?"

"I've got my reasons; there's no point in going into them now. The point is, the Tucci Family controls an empire out here. If you want it, I and the men I represent will support you. You'll have all our help in getting started, learning the business. I know it's not what you had in mind but—what's so funny?"

"You are," said Bobby. "You actually think I'd consider becoming a mobster? Aside from the fact that I'd probably get myself killed in about ten minutes, it'd be a giant drag. I'd have to spend all my time with scumbags like Relli and Catello and my mother and you. Forget it."

Patti remained impassive. "That's your final word?"

"No, my next-to-final one. My final word is 'off.' As in 'Fuck off.' "

Chapter
Twenty-
nine

TOMMY NICCOLA TOOK Annette's call in the sauna. "Can you come in for a celebration dinner on Saturday night?" she asked.

"Why not come here?"

"Johnny Baldini's preparing something really special," she said. "Besides, I want Bobby to be there."

"Bobby can't get on a plane?"

"Bobby and I haven't been getting along," said Annette. "I didn't want to worry you, but he's not himself. The other day he cursed me."

"Your own son cursed you?" said Tommy, incredulous.

"In public," said Annette. "I know he's all wound up, what with Vittorio dying and all, but he's getting out of control. Lately he's been spending most of his time with a kike sharpie named Mendy Pearlstein."

"Mendy the Pearl?"

"You know him?"

"I've seen him around over the years. He used to hang out in Chicago with Sam Giancana's cousin Mel. Strictly small change."

"I want to make things right between Bobby and me," said Annette, "but he won't listen. I wish you'd call and invite him for Saturday. He won't say no to you."

"Yeah, I suppose I could do that," said Tommy. "After all, you been such a sweet girl lately. Ralph and Jo-Jo say you did great."

"It was your plan," she said. "I just followed it. Are you gonna tell me what happened afterwards?"

"Not on the phone," said Tommy. "Wait till Saturday."

Tommy hung up, poured himself a grappa, and switched on the news. Still no word that Hoffa was missing. By tomorrow there'd be cops looking for Little Jimmy all over southern Michigan. In a week the FBI would mount a nationwide dragnet. The idea made Tommy grunt with pleasure; he didn't care if they brought in the marines, nobody was gonna find the body.

The plan had been simple, really. Ralph and Jo-Jo collected the body bag from Annette, put it in the trunk of their Cadillac, and drove to Chicago, straight to the Molinari Funeral Home, which was owned by the Niccola Family. They handed the body over to Louie Molinari, who switched it with the corpse of a seventeen-year-old killed in a car accident. The kid was so badly mutilated he was due for a closed-casket funeral. The burial went as scheduled, except that the casket contained Jimmy Hoffa.

"The boss is a fuckin' genius," Ralph said to Jo-Jo on the way home. "Nobody's gonna look for a guy in somebody else's grave."

BOBBY PUT DOWN the phone and said to Tillie, "That was Grampa No-Neck. I'm being summoned to my mother's on Saturday night to, quote, make the peace, unquote. You're finally going to meet dear old Mom."

"I'm invited?"

"I told him the only way I'd come is if you and Mendy do."

"Mendy? Why Mendy?"

"It's a balance-of-forces thing. Knowing my mother and my grandfather, they're going to gang up on me."

"Why not just blow them off, then?"

"I hate to say this, but they're the only family I've got. I don't have to like them, but I do have to go. Besides, I'm curious."

"What do you think they want?"

Bobby shrugged. "Maybe they want me to move to Chicago. Or give up the Tucci Foundation. Or tattoo 'Mother I Love You' on my biceps. Whatever it is, the answer is going to be no. And the Niccolas don't like no."

"In other words, you expect an ass-kicking and you want us there as bodyguards," said Tillie.

"Soul guards," said Bobby. "They're not interested in my body."

"Tillie Tilman, Soul Guard. It's got a ring to it. What do you wear to a mafia family drama?"

"A great big silver cross."

"I'm not pretending I'm Catholic, if that's what you want."

"Hell no. For protection."

"Protection from what?"

Bobby grinned without humor and said, "Vampires."

LEON MITSAKAWA WAS at his desk reading about the Tigers' 9–0 defeat at the hands of the Yankees when his bodyguard, Henry, brought Johnny Baldini in. He had been expecting Baldini. When he had called Annette Tucci to tell her the fugu had arrived, she had told him Baldini would be out to pick it up. "Give him my little package separately," she instructed. "Tell him it's a pair of diamond earrings."

Mitsakawa had been doing business with the Tuccis for five years, ever since the Tokyo syndicate sent him, very much against his will, to Detroit. From his office near the world headquarters of General Motors he imported food and supplies for the restaurants that catered to visiting Japanese engineers and auto executives. He also provided the ex-pats with other services. He took their bets on sporting events, sold them cocaine and heroin, and found them big-busted American women or young American boys. He had never before been asked to import fugu, but he was more than glad to do it. Without the sufferance of the Tuccis, he would find it much more difficult—and dangerous—to make his living.

The large vacuum pack from Japan contained five pounds of expertly cut, perfectly safe fish; $2,100 with shipping. The small box cost twice as much. It held two hundred grams of sliced, toxic fugu liver—enough to lethally poison half a dozen people. Mitsakawa had been ten years old when the Americans bombed Nagasaki, leaving him an orphan. Importing a Japanese fish to wipe out Americans was, to him, an ironic pleasure.

Mitsakawa handed the packages to Baldini and said, "I understand you are a great chef. I envy your guests."

Baldini flushed; he loved compliments. "What's in this little one?" he asked.

"A piece of jewelry for Mrs. Tucci," Mitsakawa lied smoothly. "A token of my esteem. She is a remarkable woman."

"She sure is," Baldini said, and frowned. Lately he had barely seen Annette. Even when they cooked together she had been distant and uncommunicative. Then, suddenly, the fugu arrived, and a change had come over her. She was excited, almost giddy, and once again affectionate. Baldini knew she was counting on him, and he wouldn't let her down; on Saturday night he would cook the greatest meal of his life. He left Mitsakawa's cramped office with a light step and drove Annette's T-Bird back to St. Clair Shores whistling Puccini. It never occurred to him that he was being followed, but even if it had, he never would have spotted Nobody Nussbaum.

Annette's was quiet and almost dark when Baldini arrived; she sat on a sofa stroking Scratch, who purred on her lap in a way that gave Baldini a jolt of irrational jealousy. He tapped one of the boxes and said, "I've got it."

Annette looked up; her brown eyes were soft, unfocused. "You're a sweet boy," she said. "Come over here."

Baldini swallowed hard. His palms were wet. As he approached he saw her skirt was above her knees. She was not wearing panties. "Come and kiss the cat," she said huskily.

It was kinky, even for Annette, but Baldini was beyond caring. He plucked up Scratch and planted a kiss on his strenuously resisting mouth.

"Let go of him, you idiot," snapped Annette.

"You said—"

"Jesus, Joseph, and Mary!" Annette caught herself, took a deep breath, and said, "I'm sorry, baby. You go get naked. Mama's gonna take good care of you."

Scratch hissed at him as he went, humbled but hopeful, into the bedroom. Annette watched him with a combination of mirth and contempt. Johnny was a gifted cook, but he was also a complete clod. For the next twenty-four hours she intended to make sure he was a happy clod. After that—well, there wasn't going to be an after that for Johnny Baldini.

Chapter Thirty

MENDY RANG THE doorbell at a quarter to seven, his arms full of long-stem roses and a bottle of chilled champagne. Annette welcomed him with a smile that stopped at her eyes.

"Jeez, you got a terrific spot here," said Mendy. Although he had known Roberto all his life, he had never been to the big house on the lake.

Annette took the champagne, the flowers, and his fedora and ushered Mendy into the living room. Bobby and Tillie smiled in welcome. Tommy raised his eyebrows.

Mendy sat on a couch next to Scratch, who was wearing a diamond collar for the occasion. "Jeez, he's a beauty," Mendy said, stroking him softly. "Abyssinian?"

"Yes. Are you a cat lover?" said Annette.

"From way back. I once had an employer named Jew Mary used to keep cats. I used to take care of 'em for her."

Tommy snorted; guys who took care of whorehouse cats weren't in his social class.

"Can I get you a drink?" asked Annette.

"J&B, Jewish booze. Hey, Don Tomás. How's tricks in the Windy City?"

"I'm going back tomorrow," said Tommy. The party had barely started, and he was bored already. Bobby had always been a strange, distant kid, and tonight he seemed glazed over. His girl was a looker, but she kept staring at Annette, making Tommy wonder if she might not be a lez. He had heard someplace that it was common among hippies. He wanted nothing more than to get dinner over with and fly back to the real world.

Bobby's stomach churned as he watched his mother pour Mendy's drink. When Bobby had arrived, twenty minutes earlier, she had startled him with a rare kiss on the cheek and an even rarer apology. "I went too far the other day," she said. "I'm sorry. Truce?"

"Truce," Bobby had mumbled, wondering how stoned he really was.

Then Annette had completed his astonishment by turning to Tillie and saying, "You're lovely. I've been looking forward to meeting you for a long time."

Now Annette handed Mendy his drink and said, "We've got a treat for dinner. Johnny Baldini's prepared a Japanese feast."

"Is that like Chinese?" asked Tommy.

"You'll love it," said Annette. "The fish alone costs four hundred dollars a pound."

Tommy brightened. "Four hundred bucks? Leave it to my baby."

Annette smiled and raised her glass. "I propose a toast. To harmony in the family. The most important thing."

They drank and Mendy said, "Where's the powder room?"

"Down the hall on the left, next to the kitchen."

"I'll find it," said Mendy. He ambled down the hall, past the bathroom to the kitchen, stuck his head in, and saw a large, soft, flushed young man in a white apron. "You must be Chef Baldini," he said. "I'm Mendy Pearlstein. Smells delicious."

"Thanks," said Johnny shyly.

"You and me are in the same racket. You ever hear of the Bull Pen Deli?"

Baldini shook his head.

"It's over by the ballpark on Michigan Avenue. Stop by anytime, I'll fix you somethin' good. Not that I'm in your league. Vittorio used to say I was the worst cook in Detroit, and that you're the best."

"Did he really say that? About me, I mean?"

"What, I'm gonna make up a thing like that? Hey, I hear you're cookin' up a special Japanese fish."

"It's called fugu," said Baldini. "It's a pufferfish."

"Jeez, I never even heard of it."

"They don't sell it in America," said Baldini. "I'm serving it two ways, as sushi and then poached."

"I hate to show my ignorance all over again, but what's sushi?"

"These," said Baldini, pointing to a serving platter of little rice cakes topped with fish. Some were decorated with cucumber, some with avocado.

Mendy eyed the platter suspiciously and said, "They ain't raw, right?"

"Actually, they shouldn't be cut until just before serving, to keep them totally fresh, but Annette insisted on preparing the sushi herself, and she wanted to get it done before you arrived."

"Don't worry, nobody will know the difference," Mendy said. "That's my motto as a cook. What's that over there?"

"It's called a microwave oven," said Baldini, frowning. "It's used for heating soup."

"How does it work?"

Baldini turned to demonstrate. As he did, Mendy quietly slipped two pieces of sushi into the pocket of his yellow sport jacket.

"Hey, I'm gonna get outta your way," he said. "I know how I feel when some buttinsky comes in the kitchen while I'm workin'. Besides, I gotta go empty my bladder."

WHEN MENDY RETURNED to the living room, Tommy looked at his Rolex, scowled, and said, "Whaddya, got prostate trouble?"

Mendy ducked his head and blinked. "My age, what don't I got? I stopped by the kitchen to pay my respects to Chef Baldini."

Annette frowned. "You know him?"

"Just his rep. He's a well-known guy in the food business. He showed me the fuju fish."

"Fugu," said Annette.

"Fugu. Right. Hey, what'd I miss?"

"We've been trying to get these two to talk about what they're going to do after college," said Annette. "Right, Dad?"

Tommy nodded. It didn't look to Mendy like he had been trying too hard.

"They're being so damn secretive," Annette said, "I think there's a wedding in the air."

"You a Catholic?" Tommy barked at Tillie. He couldn't have cared less, but he recognized that, as family patriarch, it was his place to interrogate her.

"I'm an atheist."

"Me, too," said Bobby.

"Jeez, I never knew that," said Mendy, stroking Scratch.

"That's stupid," said Tommy. "If there's no God, who invented odds?"

Annette nodded emphatically. "Exactly right."

"Hey, I'm hungry," said Tommy. "How's about some of this million-dollar fish of yours?"

Annette took a deep breath and ran over her dinner plans. First, the soup, then the sushi, avocado for her and her father, cucumber for Bobby and his friends. Within a few minutes of the first bite they'd feel a tingling on their tongues and dizziness, their throats would choke shut, and fatal paralysis would quickly set in.

The medics, when they arrived, would be sympathetic to the grieving mother. So would the police. Naturally they would want to know who procured and prepared the poison fish. Reluctantly she would name Johnny Baldini. Poor Johnny. Ironically, tragically, he too would be dead, a victim of his own negligence. A mother's tears would roll as she told the detectives that Bobby and Tillie were wonderful kids with their whole lives ahead of them. If only Johnny had been more careful. If only she had served perch.

Annette rose and clapped her hands. "Okay, dinnertime," she said. She led them into the dining room, seated them, and went to the kitchen. While she was gone Mendy slipped the two small pieces of fugu from his pocket and offered them to a grateful Scratch.

In the kitchen Baldini said, "I wish you would have let me bring in a serving girl at least."

Annette kissed him passionately and said, "If you had, we couldn't do this between courses." Then she carried the soup to the dining room.

Tommy was the first to comment on the miso. "Your cook forgot the meat and vegetables," he said.

"It's supposed to be a light broth," said Annette.

"What's this stuff floating around?"

"It's called tofu."

"I think it's delicious," said Tillie.

"Me too," said Bobby, to annoy his grandfather.

"Atheist soup," Tommy grumbled.

"They just opened a Japanese restaurant in Ann Arbor," said Tillie.

"Yeah, they're springin' up," Mendy said. "It's gonna be popular I bet."

"Never catch on," Tommy said. "Not with crappy soup like this."

"There's a saying my mother had," Mendy said. "About food and smell, you can't argue." The others looked at him blankly, and he shrugged. "In Yiddish it rhymes."

Bobby grinned. "That what you tell your customers when they complain?"

"I've used it once or twice," said Mendy.

Annette began collecting the empty bowls. "Now for the sushi," she announced gaily.

Johnny Baldini greeted her with a needy expression. Once again she kissed him passionately. Then slowly, teasingly, she slid a piece of fugu-and-cucumber sushi into his helpless mouth and whispered, "We'll have some fun when they leave."

Suddenly they heard a high-pitched choking sound. Annette rushed into the dining room and saw Mendy Pearlstein kneeling next to Scratch, who was lying motionless on the floor. Frantically she placed her ear against the cat's chest. When she looked up at Mendy there were tears in her eyes. "He's gone," she said.

"He was fine a minute ago," said Bobby.

"What, he's dead now so he shoulda been dead a minute ago?" said Tommy. "That makes a lotta sense."

"Could be something he ate," said Tillie.

"That's impossible," said Annette. "Nobody feeds him but me."

There was a pause and then Mendy said, "Well . . . "

Annette saw the look on his face and snarled, "What did you do, you crazy old bastard?"

"I just gave him a piece of the fugu," said Mendy. "I mean, how often does a cat get to eat a high-class fish like that?"

"You did what?" she shrieked.

"Jeez," said Mendy. "It was dinner. I didn't know it was poison."

Bobby and Tillie exchanged a look. Bobby said, "*You* did, though. You knew, didn't you, Mom?"

"Hey," said Tommy. "That's your mother you're talking to."

Bobby ignored him. "How about it, Mom? Cook some poison fish for your nearest and dearest?"

Tommy jumped up, grabbed Bobby with one hand, and swung with the other, a short, powerful right to the face. Blood spurted from Bobby's nose. "Don't you ever talk to your mother that way," he said. "Where's that fuckin' cook?"

"It's not Baldini's fault," said Annette. "Scratch was allergic to fish."

"Bullshit," said Bobby. "He ate fish all the time."

Tommy shot Bobby a murderous look. "Curse your mother again, and I'll break your back," he said. Then he charged into the kitchen. There on the floor, a horrible grimace on his face, lay Johnny Baldini.

"Him I didn't feed," said Mendy.

"Maybe he's allergic to fish too," said Bobby.

Tommy started for Bobby, but Mendy seized his arm in an intentionally painful grip. "He's your grandson, Don Tomás," he said with soft reproach. "You don't want to hit him again."

"You don't see what's going on?" Bobby yelled at Tommy. "Are you that fucking stupid?"

"He's crazy," Annette said. "Baldini made the sushi. What did he do, poison himself?"

"Hey," said Mendy, "he told me you fixed it." Annette glared at him, and he put his gnarled hand on his heart. "Honest."

"Is that right?" asked Tommy.

"The sushi's fine," said Annette. "Here, look." She grabbed a piece from the cutting board and gobbled it down.

"Try one with the cucumber," said Mendy.

"Fuck you," said Annette. "I don't have to prove anything to you. Get the hell out of my house. And take my son and his atheist whore with you."

"Eat the one with the cucumbers," said Tommy.

"What?" said Annette.

"Eat the one with the cucumbers. Show these jerks how full of shit they are."

"No," said Annette. "I consider that an insult."

"What, you think I don't trust my own daughter? Give me one, I'll eat it."

Tillie plucked a piece of sushi from the cutting board and handed it to him, but Annette snatched it away.

"What's the matter with you?" asked Tommy.

"How many times do you have to hear it?" said Bobby. "She was going to poison us."

"Not you," Annette said to her father. "Bobby and Pearlstein made a deal with the National Commission. They were going to take over the Family, leave us out in the cold. You would have lost the Center Cut."

"I'm calling the cops," said Bobby.

"No cops," snapped Tommy. "What the hell's the matter with you?"

"It ain't his fault, Don Tomás," said Mendy. "He don't know no better, he's a straight kid. You think a kid like him's gonna make a deal with the National Commission?"

Tommy stared at his grandson. Then he said, "You three, get outta here. Don't talk to nobody. G'won."

"I'm not letting her get away with this," said Bobby.

Mendy took him by the elbow and said, "Come on, Bobby, this ain't between us anymore. Let's go get some salami and eggs."

"And smoke a jay," said Tillie. "Jesus, Bobby. No wonder you didn't want to introduce me to your family."

WHEN THEY WERE alone Tommy said, "You were going to kill Bobby."

"You can't stand Bobby. You never could."

"He's blood," said Tommy. "My only male heir."

"So what? You never cared about that Sicilian son-worship crap. You always treated me like an equal. That's what I love most about you."

"Good. That means you understand why you gotta eat the sushi. I'd say the same thing to a son."

"What?"

"I hate repeating myself," said Tommy the Neck.

"Daddy—"

"Don't Daddy me, Annette. You did the Hoffa job, I give you all the credit. But on this here, you fucked up very bad. We got a dead body in your kitchen and no explanation. The cops start investigating, it opens up a can of worms. It's gotta end with you. Then all we got is a cooking accident."

"We can ditch the body—"

"You left three witnesses."

"Don't worry, I'll take care of them."

"I can't afford a war in Detroit between you and Bobby. I promised the Commission I'd keep the peace."

"You *what*?"

"Yeah," said Tommy. "I cut a deal with Don Polumba. I do Hoffa and Detroit comes under me."

"Under *us*," said Annette. "*I'm* the one who did Hoffa. I did him for you and me, the Niccolas. We're in this together."

Tommy shook his head. "You're a mother who was gonna kill her own son. How can I trust you?"

"So you're gonna kill me instead?"

"I ain't a mother," said Tommy. He reached out and grabbed Annette by the hair, pulling her toward him. "Eat the fuckin' fish, Annette."

Annette slithered out of his grip and grabbed a sashimi knife from the cutting board. Tommy smashed her hand on the counter, and the knife fell to the floor. With brutal strength he locked her head under his left arm and, as she flailed at him, pried her lips apart with his stubby fingers and forced eight hundred dollars' worth of fugu down his daughter's throat.

TEN DAYS AFTER the disappearance of Jimmy Hoffa, Annette Tucci was laid to rest in a private ceremony attended by Bobby and Tillie, Mendy, Ann Tillman, Rudy, and Mouse Campanella.

Tommy the Neck wasn't there. The day after he returned to Chicago he was gunned down in the street near Wrigley Field. His bodyguards, Jo-Jo and Ralph, died too, taking the secret of Jimmy Hoffa's final resting place with them.

Tommy's funeral was the biggest event in the history of the Illinois floral industry. The single largest wreath came from Carmine Patti, who was now unhappily installed as the National Commission's caretaker in Detroit. His card read: "Last respects to a man whose reach truly exceeded his grasp."

Annette Tucci's ceremony was, by contrast, modest to the point of being spartan. All that was left of her was an urn of ashes. After the cremation, when they all repaired to the Bull Pen for a memorial meal of brisket and mashed potatoes, Bobby placed the urn on the counter. Ann Tillman peered into it and said, "There doesn't seem to be very much there. She must have been a tiny woman."

"She was on a diet at the time of her death," said Bobby.

Ann frowned and said, "What are you going to do with the remains?"

"Donate them to veterinary science. A professor in Ann Arbor is going to turn her into experimental kitty litter."

"How awful," said Ann.

"It's what she would have wanted," said Bobby.

Mendy said, "I know you guys are atheists, but I still think we should have had a clergyman present. Too bad Lips Lipsky ain't around."

"Lips Lipsky," Rudy said, rolling the name off his tongue with anticipation. "Tell us about Lips Lipsky."

"Lips was the rabbi of the wiseguys' shul back during Pro'bition. He only had two rules—never talk to the cops, and never lie to God. Very holy guy."

"My man," said Rudy. "Mendy the Pearl, got him a memory for every damn occasion."

"I suppose I should be shocked," said Ann Tillman. "After all, I am a mother. But I'm not shocked. In fact, I'm amused. Aren't I awful?"

"I still can't believe you're going to Rio," said Tillie.

"It is a cliché, I know, but I've always wanted to go to Carnival. Your father was always too busy with his Swiss floozies to take me. But now I've taken him, in a manner of speaking." She squeezed Mendy's arm affectionately. "I do wish you'd come with."

"Aw, what am I gonna do down there?" said Mendy. "I don't even speak Brazilian. Besides, me and Rudy got work to do."

"Like what?" asked Mouse.

"Education," said Rudy. "You lookin' at the president of the Oakland Avenue People's Academy. And this here is Professor Pearlstein, academic dean."

"What's the scam?" asked Mouse.

"Its no scam, my man. The People's Academy has been established to convey the experience and skills of previous generations to the untrained youth of the inner city."

"Yeah," said Mendy, a sparkle in his eyes. "It's a chance to give something to the community besides heartburn and gas."

"A vocational school for gangsters?" said Tillie. "Cool."

"We refer to it as practical criminology," said Rudy. "I got that from the lady at the Ford Foundation. Along with one million, three hundred thousand dollars."

"You gonna be turnin' out your own wiseguys," said Mouse. "Hey, you planning on taking Italians?"

"Certainly," said Rudy. "Fostering interethnic relations is a part of our mandate."

Bobby said, "I'm hurt you guys went to the Ford Foundation. What's wrong with the Roberto Tucci Foundation? Mendy's a trustee, after all."

"Aw, you got better things to do with your dough," said Mendy. "Besides, I'm resigning—I'm gonna be too busy teachin' school. Tillie, why don't you take my slot?"

"Me? I don't know the first thing about being a trustee."

"Aw, it's a snap. I done it at Jackson. All you gotta do is not run away."

Tillie ruffled Bobby's long hair and said, "I'm not splitting. This is where the action is."

After lunch Rudy left for a meeting with Delbert, who was chairman of the tenure committee; Mouse went to the Tucci Building to tell Carmine Patti what he had learned; and Tillie drove her mother out to Bloomfield Hills. When they were alone, Bobby said to Mendy, "How did you know?"

"Know what?"

"That the fish was poisoned. How could you know that?"

"Hey, I'm a chef, don't forget," said Mendy. "I know bad fish when I see it."

Bobby shook his head. "Bad lox, maybe. I'll bet you never even heard of fugu before the other night."

Mendy grinned. "You're turning into a shrewdie," he said. "Your grampa would be proud of you."

"You didn't answer my question though," said Bobby. "How you knew."

"I got lucky with a coincidence. This guy I know, Nobody Nussbaum, they call him that on accounta he's got a forgettable face, he was trailing your mom's car when Baldini drove it over to Leon Mitsakawa's place."

"Who's he?"

"A Japanese fella, very nice guy. Him and me have scalped tickets together a few times. He's the one told me about the fugu. Course he didn't tell me who it was for, but I put one and one together."

Bobby laughed. "Mendy the Pearl. Well, you said you'd have a home-court advantage in Detroit."

"You live in a place this long, it figures you're gonna know people."

Bobby lit a joint and took a deep hit. "This has been some summer," he said. "Are you really going into this school thing?"

"Why not?"

"How'd you like a music teacher?"

"Sure. Your band can play at the junior prom," said Mendy.

"Seriously, I could help out—"

"Aw, you got better things to do with your life."

"I'm not talking about forever. But I feel like there's still some things I can learn."

"From me? Nah, I got nothin' left to learn you—you already know what it took me all my life to figure out. And the funny thing is, you got it from her," he said, tapping the urn.

"Got what?"

"The golden rule," said Mendy. "Live by the fish, die by the fish."

"That's it? Live by the fish, die by the fish?"

Mendy smiled and said, "What were you expecting, Shakespeare? Hey, go catch up with Tillie."

"Aw," said Bobby.

"Aw yourself," Mendy said. "And don't forget to stop by now and then. I'll fix you somethin' good to eat."

About the Author

WILLIAM WOLF is the pseudonym of a journalist and author who wishes to remain anonymous. His reluctance to reveal his true identity is unrelated to anything he may know about the actual events surrounding the disappearance of Jimmy Hoffa. Really.